MW01670773

The African-American

By JERRY EVANS

Magnum Press
Oklahoma

For My People

Other Novels by Jerry Evans

Karate Master

Karate Master II

Karate Master III

Jack Ward

The Caretaker

©copyright 1993 by Jerry Evans

Magnum Press
Stillwater, Oklahoma

All rights reserved. No part of this book may be reproduced or utilized in any form or by any means, electronic or mechanical, including video, photocopying, recording, or by any information storage or retrieval system without permission from the publisher.

Manufactured in the United States.

Library of Congress Catalog Card Number: 93-079055
ISBN: 0-9623698-8-8

Chapter One

Ulysses Dupree stood in the picture window of the old abandoned house, shivering and looking across the street at the run-down elementary school. The school was surrounded by slum housing. He then glanced into the dreary afternoon sky, shot through with rain clouds and threatening of thunderstorms. When Sammy racked back the slide of his .22 automatic pistol and chambered a cartridge, Ulysses frowned.

"Put it away. I told you this ain't a shooting. Didn't I tell you that?" He stared into Sammy's big-eyed, dark-complected, hatchet face.

"What the hell you talking about?" Sammy turned to Mo.

Mo rolled his beady eyes, gave a fat-jawed grimace, and threw up his hands.

"The Cyclops raped your sister, Man!" Sammy spat, gazing into Ulysses's handsome brown face. "He raped Gwen!"

"I know that! Don't you think I know that?" Ulysses shouted. "Ain't I sat up with her, too, while she bawled and threatened to kill herself?"

Sammy rolled his eyes and put the gun away.

Ulysses glanced back out at the trees whipping in the

late-autumn wind, as forked lightning flashed across the sky, etching beautiful, veined patterns. No cars or people were out in the cold as golden-brown leaves scattered through the air. When he heard Mo's switchblade pop open, he looked at the heavy-set, dark-complected youth and sighed. Mo grinned and began cleaning his nails with the point of the blade, as he struck up a low whistle.

"This ain't a cutting, either," Ulysses uttered.

"Well, just what the hell is it, then?" Mo asked, gazing into Ulysses's warmly-expressive eyes and intelligent-looking face. Mo then looked at Sammy, who sighed and shook his head.

"How in the devil are we supposed to deal with the Cyclops, then?" Mo frowned. "Shit, he's at least seven feet tall and weighs over two hundred and seventy pounds."

Ulysses tossed his buddies a couple of brass knuckles from his jacket pocket.

Mo cried, "You got to be kidding! You know how close we got to get to use these?"

"Well, there are three of us," Ulysses snapped. "And the Cyclops's only got one eye. So that ought to make it just about even."

"Even, hell! Shit, Man, you crazy!" Sammy blew up. "The ape's built like goddamn King Kong!"

"You cats cuss too much, Man!" Ulysses frowned. "Now, listen, if y'all don't want to help me, go on home. Just don't stand around bitching about it. I'll tackle him by himself."

"You'll what? Don't make me laugh," Mo scoffed. "What chance would *you* have?"

"Maybe none. But I got to do *something.* And I ain't no murderer. I can't kill nobody. My mama didn't raise me that way." Ulysses looked off.

"Who said anything about killing him?" Sammy's voice

rose. "Just let me put a couple in his knees," he patted his pistol, "and give us a snowman's chance in hell."

Ulysses looked at the tall, lean youth, and Sammy grinned and looked away.

"Naw, Man, it's your show, and we together," Mo sighed. "All for one. Just like always. We been through a hell of a lot of shit together, and this don't change nothing. Right, Sammy?"

"Right on, Homie." Sammy shook his fist, cracked a smile, and placed his hand on Ulysses's shoulder. "We together — even in the hospital, Bro."

Ulysses knocked his hand away, and he laughed.

"Yeah," Mo brightened. "Maybe we can get beds side by side."

"Or grave sites," Sammy threw out.

"I don't see why not," Mo shrugged.

Perturbed, Ulysses looked at them, and they smirked.

A moment of silence passed.

"What did the Cyclops go to see, anyway?" Ulysses asked, firing up a cigarette.

"I don't know, Man, but I think it was a gangster movie or something," Sammy answered.

"Yeah, that would suit him — being the two-bit hoodlum he is," Ulysses frowned.

"Picture should be over by now." Mo looked at his watch.

"Yeah, he'll be along directly." Ulysses drew on his cigarette and glanced back through the boarded-up, fire-gutted house. Four rays of sacred-looking light struck through here and there in burnt-through places, revealing that the old, two-story house had once been a proud and noble structure, during another age and time.

"Say, Man," Sammy broke out, "why didn't y'all have the Cyclops arrested?"

"Dr. Johnson said it wouldn't do no good. By the time he examined Gwen, she had taken a bath and washed all the evidence away."

"He didn't leave no marks on her?" Mo asked.

"No. She didn't fight him." Ulysses dropped his head and shook it. "Wouldn't have done no good, no way. Just made it worse."

"Yeah," Mo sighed.

They stood watch in silence again.

Mo cleared his throat. "You thought about how we gonna deal with the Philistines, Man, if we get past the Cyclops?"

"Naw, he ain't thought about it," Sammy sneered, peering back out the window, "'cause we ain't gonna get past the Cyclops — not without shooting his ass."

"Now, listen. Three pit bulls can whip any dog. I don't care how big the sucker is," Ulysses gnashed. "But you got to hit like a pit bull — hard, fast, and furious!"

"Yeah, but pit bulls got to be crazy in the fucking head to go against a goddamn grizzly bear," Mo scoffed.

Ulysses ignored him. "But look to get hurt, too, 'cause we definitely gonna get hurt." He let the smoke crawl out of his mouth.

"You got to tell us *that!*" Sammy cried.

Ulysses gritted his teeth. "But we gonna pull him down, Jack — just like David brought down Goliath. And that's the main thing!"

He looked back out at the dilapidated tabernacle church standing across the street from the school, as he felt a lump in his throat and felt his stomach tied in knots. Homing pigeons returned to the roofs of both buildings, and the old man who now swept down the church steps stopped to give a stray cat a bowl of milk. The cat had black, brown, and white markings, and the old man petted it.

"We supposed to graduate in May," Sammy thought out loud. "A scout even came by to talk to me about a football scholarship to college."

"You can forget that," Mo uttered, putting a stick of gum in his mouth and offering the pack around.

"Now, listen," Ulysses barked, "it's because ain't nobody suppose to chop down the Cyclops that when we do, they'll think twice about avenging him, especially because we ain't cut or shot him for what he did to my sister, and they know I got a right to."

"You think that's gonna make any difference to the Philistines, Man?" Mo exclaimed. "You think that's gonna make any difference? Shit, grow up!"

"There he comes!" Sammy's voice was suddenly charged.

Ulysses clenched his teeth, zipped up his leather jacket, and drew brass knucks on either hand.

"All right, let's take him," he grimaced, as his heart pounded. "Just like we practiced. No holding back. All right?" He mashed his cigarette butt.

They all looked at each other anxiously, and his companions nodded their heads.

They headed out to meet the Cyclops on the school yard.

Chapter Two

As they approached the brute, encircling him on all sides, Ulysses looked up into his ugly, dark-complected face, — a face marked by crude features, scars, stubby teeth, and a put-out left eye. The Cyclops, wearing a snug corduroy jacket that showed off the bulge of his muscles, stopped, and his face broke into a cruel grin at the sight of Ulysses. Dupree stood shaking with hate and fear as he stared up at the massive beast.

"You raped my sister, Cyclops!" he seethed.

"Uh-hunh," he grinned. "But you know I don't allow nobody to call me that!" he drawled. "I'm gonna kick your ass now!" he pointed. "Yeah, I raped the bitch. Sure was good, too. Gonna get me some more of that, real soon."

"Like hell you are!" Ulysses cried, charging him and throwing dirt in his face. Cursing in rage, the Cyclops brought his hands up to his blinded eye, and Ulysses kicked him in the groin and cracked him in the jaw with the brass knucks. The giant cried out as his head snapped to one side and his body reeled. Sammy then caught him in the face again and knocked him toward Mo, who tore into him with blows to the nose and mouth.

Bellowing in rage and pain and pouring blood from his nose and mouth, the Cyclops struck out blindly and caught

Mo in the face, knocking him sprawling and unconscious. Ulysses then laid into the hulk from behind, driving blows into his spine and kidneys. Snarling and grunting, the Cyclops wheeled, grabbing Ulysses in a bear hug and nearly squeezing the life out of him. Dupree hollered, almost passing out, as all of his six feet one hundred and eighty pounds was hoisted into the air over the Cyclops's head. Kicking and writhing, he felt the vise-grip hands suddenly give way as Sammy tackled the ogre, hitting him hard and cutting him off at the knees. Ulysses crashed to the ground, rolled, and lay senseless.

Hearing his friend hollering for help as he and the Cyclops tussled on the ground, Ulysses looked over and saw the giant roll on top of Sammy, grabbing his head and pounding it into the ground. Reaching way down into his guts, Dupree gathered his strength and struggled back to his feet. He then staggered back to the dinosaur and drove the heel of his shoe into the back of the beast's head. When the Cyclops fell forward off of Sammy, Ulysses kicked him again, then dropped on top of him and with the brass knucks hammered right and left hooks into his face. The Cyclops's head snapped back and forth under the impact of the punches, as he was knocked cold.

Rolling off of him, Ulysses sat there, breathing hard and trying to gather his strength. He looked at his companions, who were still passed out, as pain spread through his ribs and back and moved up into his shoulders.

"God!" he uttered, wiping the cold sweat and shaking off his pain. "Damn!" Then a big smile spread across his face. He looked around. No one was in sight. Suddenly there was thunder and wind in the trees. As golden-yellow leaves flurried through the air, the rain began to fall, and Ulysses looked up at it.

Mo struggled into a sitting position. "Did we get him?"

he groaned.

Ulysses nodded his head and pointed. "Damn straight we did, Bro."

Sammy then moaned and sat up. He held his head, looking around dazed as the rain whipped his face.

"How do you feel, Blood?" Ulysses asked.

Sammy looked at the Cyclops and shook his head.

"Damn! I still hear birds singing! Anybody got any aspirins? Extra-strength?" he asked, and they all laughed, getting to their feet. They went over and looked down at the beast.

"Didn't I tell you?" Ulysses uttered as the cold rain soaked him. "Didn't I tell you?"

They all looked at each other and grinned.

"Come on, let's go home," he said, shivering, and the three friends trudged off together.

CHAPTER THREE

When Ulysses got home at dinnertime, his mother was setting the table, and the kitchen was filled with the delicious aroma of food.

"Hi, Mama," he said, putting his coat on the back of the kitchen chair. "What's for dinner?" He went over and looked in the pots. "Mmmm," he smiled at his plump, attractive, brown-complected, fifty-year-old mother. "My favorite."

Smiling back she continued setting the table and humming 'Swing low, Sweet Chariot.'

"Where you been, Boy? You all wet."

"Just messing around with Mo and Sammy. How's Gwen?" he asked, sitting down and glancing thoughtfully around the homey little kitchen, with its drab-looking cabinets and walls, scarred-up floor, and time-worn appliances.

Mrs. Dupree stopped and frowned. "She's still in her shell and don't want to eat. She got to eat something, though. She ain't eat in two days. Just lay in bed and stare up at the ceiling. I'm real worried about her, U. Dr. Johnson said he would stop by again today and that she might need to see a psychiatrist, but we can't afford no psychiatrist. Go in and try again to have her come in and eat a little something."

Ulysses shook his head and proceeded through their clean but poorly-furnished, three-bedroom, frame house. He knocked on her door. There was no answer. Calling his twin sister's name softly, he eased the door open and peeped in. She lay in bed with the lights out and her face turned away. Ulysses went over and sat beside her.

"How you doing, Honey?"

"All right," she muttered.

"Mama wants you to come and eat a little something."

"Ain't hungry."

"But you got to eat *something.*" Turning her head toward him, he stroked her long, dark hair tenderly and gazed into her lovely, seventeen-year-old, peach-complected face. "Please! For me," he coaxed. "I love you, Honey. I don't want to see you waste away like this."

She stared, withdrawn, into space.

"I been praying for you, Honey, 'cause I love you. I love you like Absalom in *The Bible* loved his sister Tamar. Remember the story?"

She didn't say anything.

"What about Jimmy? Don't you want to live for him? He'll be home from college in a few months. You want to be pretty for him, don't you?"

She focused on her brother now, and her eyes filled with tears.

"You think he's gonna want me after this? I'm defiled! That filthy animal took my virginity, and I might even be pregnant with his beast child, for all I know. And not a damn thing is gonna be done about any of it! How do you think I feel? Oh, God! I just want to die!" She shook with anguish, and he held her.

Tears came to his eyes as he stared across the room at her vanity, bristling with cosmetics. A picture of Jimmy sat upon the bureau. He looked out handsomely and intellectually through wire-rimmed glasses. "If you pregnant, Dr. Johnson will take care of it. And this won't make no difference to

Jimmy. Not the kind of man *he* is. And another thing. You wrong, Honey. Something has been done about it."

"What?" she convulsed.

"Well, tell you what. If you'll come in and sit at the table — you don't have to eat nothing, just sit — I'll tell you. Deal?"

"He get arrested?" she sobbed.

"No."

"Then what, for God's sake? Is he dead? God, I wish to God he were dead!"

"No, he ain't dead, neither. Don't try to guess. Just come in and sit, okay? Mama needs to hear, too, I suppose."

She drew back and looked at him.

"Come on." Gently pulling her up, he led her into the kitchen.

Mrs. Dupree was both surprised and delighted as her daughter sat.

"This is a fine Sunday dinner, Mama," Ulysses complimented, looking at the pinto beans, cornbread, roast, and vegetables.

"Mama, I can't go back to school tomorrow," Gwen shook her head, gazing at her empty plate. "I can't face those people. Everybody's gonna know and be talking. . . ."

Mrs. Dupree served her daughter's plate. "What you think they gonna say, Honey, except how sorry they are?"

"I don't want their sympathy!" Gwen wiped her eyes. "And I know the way some of those boys are gonna be smirking at me. 'Well, Little Miss Stuck-up got hers. She won't be so uppity after this!' I can hear them now. And not a damn thing was done about it! So what you got to tell me?" She turned to her brother.

Having helped his plate, Ulysses reached into his jacket pocket and took out the brass knucks. They were bloodstained, and he put them on the table. His mother stopped eating and drew back. Gwen sat up.

"What you got there, Son?"

He clenched his teeth. "I can't stop them from talking when we get back to school tomorrow, Honey. But by the end of the day, they'll know that the Cyclops didn't get away with it. He paid. And I mean he paid."

"What do you mean?" his sister asked.

"It was me, Sammy, and Mo. We didn't cut or shoot him, but we busted him up good. Suspect we broke something, too."

"You all fought *him?*" Gwen exclaimed.

Her brother nodded his head.

"You didn't get hurt?"

"We a little sore, but nothing to speak of."

"Y'all used these?"

"Yeah." Ulysses ate.

"All three of you?"

"Yeah."

"You're kidding!"

"Would I kid you about a thing like that?" He looked at her. Gwen shook her head as sudden joy and disbelief worked in her face. Mrs. Dupree sat, stricken.

Ulysses put the knucks away.

"Like I said, I can't stop people from gossiping, but I guarantee you nobody'll be laughing. Everybody's scared of the Cyclops, see? But after this, they'll know — ain't no man can't be whipped. And ain't no man gonna do what he did to *my* sister and get away with it!"

Tears came to her eyes, and she got up, kneeled beside her brother and hugged and kissed him. "Thank you, my brother!"

Mrs. Dupree took a deep breath. Her hands were shaking.

Ulysses continued eating, as Gwen now sat staring at him.

"How you feel, Mama?" he asked.

"I don't know how I feel. Son, you started something that ain't over and ain't gonna be over until. . . . Oh, God! The Philistines ain't gonna let this go."

"They know where to find me," Ulysses said, buttering his bread.

"Ain't you scared?"

"I did what had to be done, Mama. And I'll do whatever else has to be done."

"What you mean? What you gonna do?" Mrs. Dupree's voice shook.

He smiled and patted her hand. "Same as I always done, Mama. Keep working after school and graduate in May with Gwen." He looked at his sister as she stared at him with love and respect. "Except I ain't gonna get no college scholarship, like her." Smiling, he reached over and stroked her face. "But I can work and save my money, and maybe one day — "

"Son, they ain't gonna let this go. You hear me? You gonna have the devil to pay!" Mrs. Dupree shook her head. "They ain't gonna leave you be. They gonna be laying for you."

"Let them find me then, Mama. But remember one thing — the Philistines hide behind the Cyclops. Without him, they ain't so tough. . . ."

"They ain't so . . .! Dear Lord!" Mrs. Dupree stared at the ceiling. "All my life I worked like a dog to raise my kids right and put them through school. To teach them the right values of human decency, hard work, and standing on their own two feet. Their father was killed in Viet Nam, and I done the best I knew how. But now. . . ." She flattened her hand on her heaving breast, got up, and walked out.

"Food's getting cold," Ulysses nodded at his sister as he got up from the table. Still staring at him, she picked up her fork as he went out to see about their mother.

Chapter Four

That evening Dupree stood out on the front porch of his home and looked up and down the run-down neighborhood of small brick and frame houses. A few cars streamed by as big elm and sycamore trees scattered their orange and yellow leaves everywhere. And churning in the sky, thunderclouds threatened more rain. As Ulysses filled his lungs with the fresh, clean air and gazed up at the treetops, the wind gusted through the branches with a forlorn and melancholy wail. Suspended from the porch ceiling, a cluster of wind chimes bestrewed the air with a shower of tinkling as the youth's mind was spirited away to another place and time.

The scene was from one of his favorite old movies. The hero was a cool detective who had tracked a beautiful woman to a sunny resort in Mexico while working on a case. One warm night they met on the beach, all alone, and the scene was played out against a backdrop of moonlight and impassioned music. As the wind tossed her hair and the moonlight caressed her face, the detective realized that he had fallen in love with her and would betray his client, the powerful crime boss who had commissioned him to bring her back and from whom she had run away. As the lovers smiled deep into each other's eyes, the cool blue whitecaps washed the shore at their feet, the refreshing ocean spray came off the sea, and the tide shimmered in the moonlight. Tomorrow they would brave great danger together because of their love, but tonight — as the rushing waves lashed the nearby rocky cliffs — ah, tonight . . .!

"You want to take *The Oklahoma City Gazette?"* A paperboy rode up on his bicycle.

Snapping out of his daydream, Dupree sighed and shook his head, and the boy rode on, throwing papers. Soon Dr. Johnson drove up and got out of his late-model, white Chevrolet. Ulysses smiled at the tall, thin, distinguished-looking, fifty-eight-year-old man. He was light-brown-skinned, wore a dark suit, and glasses, and had gray-streaked hair. "How's Gwen?" he asked, mounting the steps with his black bag.

"She's better."

"That's good. Has she eaten anything?"

"A little."

"That's *good!"* he exclaimed.

"Listen, Doc, I got something to tell you."

"All right."

Ulysses laid out the story about the Cyclops. The doctor stood staring down.

"You're in danger, now."

"I know."

It started to rain again, and Dupree looked out at it, then gazed at the little puddles in the yard, being dimpled by the rain.

"If there's anything I can do. . . ."

"Maybe. After it's all over."

The doctor started to speak again.

"Come on. Let's go inside," Ulysses said.

Chapter Five

Gwen and her mother were watching television when Dr. Johnson stepped into the living room.

"How's my favorite patient?" he smiled at Gwen.

"A little better," she grinned.

"Good. How are you, Mrs. Dupree?"

"Tolerably well," she smiled. "Please have a seat, Doctor."

"Thank you. Dreary afternoon, isn't it?" he asked as the thunder rumbled.

"Yes, it is," Mrs. Dupree replied.

"Listen, if you have any problems of any kind, you let me know, okay?" he said to Gwen.

She nodded her head.

"Especially let me know if you start having morbid thoughts that you can't get rid of."

"Yes, Sir."

"And keep eating a little something, okay?"

She nodded.

The doctor crossed his legs and glanced at television. A nature show was on, and a huge lion pride was stalking a herd of skittish zebras on the savannas of Africa. As the pride slowly moved in for the kill, Gwen turned the channel, and the physician looked at Mrs. Dupree, who was staring at the floor.

He and Ulysses exchanged concerned glances.

"Mrs. Dupree, Ulysses told me what happened. If there is anything I can do. . . ."

She looked at him, forced a smile, and shook her head.

"I just read my Bible and stay prayerful, Doctor. That's all I can do. I just stay prayerful."

"Yes, Ma'am. That's the thing. Prayer is wonderfully healing and comforting."

Everybody looked at the television for a moment. A sitcom was now on.

"I guess you're excited that your children are graduating in May?" The doctor smiled.

"Oh, yes, Sir! I just hope everything works out." She looked at Ulysses.

"I'm sure everything will. You know God protected Daniel in the lions' den."

"Yes, Sir. He surely did! He surely did!" she smiled.

"What college do you want to attend, U?"

"I ain't sure, Doc. I ain't gonna get no scholarship, though, and I won't have the money to go right away."

"I see. Maybe I can help. . . ."

"Oh, no. I couldn't."

"We'll talk about it later." The doctor smiled with his eyes. "What about you, Gwen? I know — you're going to Howard to be with Jimmy, aren't you?"

"Sure am," she blushed.

"He'll make a fine physician, and you'll make a fine nurse."

"Thank you. I can't wait until we finish," she brightened. "And we're gonna get as far away from here as possible." Her face hardened.

"What you mean?" Mrs. Dupree asked. "This is your home."

"This crime-ridden slum!" she scorned. "Don't make me laugh."

Mrs. Dupree and the doctor looked at each other.

"But, Honey, I live here." Mrs. Dupree objected. "This is my home."

"When I become successful, Mama, I'm moving you out of this jungle. To a nice part of town. Away from these. . . ."

Her mother cut a sharp eye at her.

"Ever occur to you that I might not want to leave my home?"

"This ain't home. This is hell. And you could sure use another house! A nice one!" Gwen frowned, glancing around the drab-looking living room, with its well-worn sofa, coffee table, and easy chair. Mrs. Dupree sat in an old platform rocker, next to the lamp table. Across the room stood a nice console television. But the carpet in front of it was threadbare.

"Good enough for you now, huh?" her mother snapped. "My home is where my people, my friends, and my roots are. I ain't moving!"

Gwen rolled her eyes and looked away. "Why are *you* down here, Dr. Johnson? You can go anywhere — so many nice places in the world. Folks here can't pay you nothing."

"I'm here because I want to be."

"Why, for God's sake? Ain't nothing here but crime, ignorance, poverty, and drug addiction."

"Is that all you see?"

"What else is there to see, for God's sake?" she cried. "No self-respecting human being would live here if he could possibly help it. Decent people can't even walk the streets."

"I walk the streets," her mother retorted. "Been walking them for years. Besides, if Jesus was alive today, where you think He'd be — in the rich neighborhoods?"

Gwen sighed and looked off.

"Have you talked to Jimmy about his plans after graduation?" the doctor asked.

"What do you mean?"

Dr. Johnson looked at Ulysses and his mother.

"I see you haven't."

"What plans?" Gwen asked.

"Perhaps I shouldn't —"

"What plans?" she insisted.

"Well," the doctor shifted his weight. "He aims to come back here and start up a clinic with me and. . . ."

Gwen exploded, "Over my dead body!" Tears sprang to her eyes. "Not if he loves me! Never! Never!" She ran out of the room.

Ulysses started to go after her.

"Leave her be!" his mother said, clutching the arms of her chair.

The doctor sighed, dropped his eyes, and shook his head. "I'm sorry. I shouldn't have — "

"Never you mind, Doctor," Mrs. Dupree raised her hand and shook it. "It's all right. She be okay."

"Yes, but I didn't mean to — "

"You ain't done nothing wrong. She be fine."

"Yes," he sighed.

"You feel the same way your sister does?" Mrs. Dupree looked at her son.

"Mama, I can understand the way Gwen feels. She been through hell. No way around it. None of us know how she feels. We ain't been raped."

His mother stared at him. "All kinds of ways to be raped, boy. Don't ever forget that!"

"Well, I'd better be going." The doctor rose. "Remember, if you need me. . . ."

"Thanks so much, Doctor, for coming and for being a

friend. It means a lot," Mrs. Dupree said as he went over, gripped her hand, and kissed her on the forehead.

"I'll see you out, Doc," Ulysses said.

As the men stood on the porch and watched the late-evening rain and occasional cars hissing by, the physician was concerned.

"I hope Gwen and Jimmy will be able to work out their differences. He's not the kind of man who can ever be happy in his own little well-to-do, self-indulgent world. He must reach out to others less fortunate. . . ."

"I know," Ulysses replied. "He's like you."

They smiled.

"It ain't easy, though," the physician sighed. "I would never pretend that it is. Sometimes I get really frustrated with all of the help our people need. And they can be so difficult at times, and even dangerous. And I do get tired. But the spiritual rewards are enormous, and God looks after me and renews me for the struggle each day."

Ulysses shook his head in admiration, touched by the healer's openness. But, he thought, if I had a medical degree, I would be a thousand miles away from here. But I sure appreciate the Doc's being here and don't know what we'd do without him.

"Anyway. . . ." The physician sighed and took a deep breath, "you may need to leave town. I've got a sister in Guthrie —"

"I'll be all right, Doc."

The doctor placed his hand on the youth's shoulder. "Just let me know if you need me. . . ."

"Sure. And thanks."

They shook hands and smiled.

Dr. Johnson then hurried through the rain to his car.

Ulysses watched him drive off, then lit a cigarette and stood for a time, gazing out at the downpour. As the lightning flashed and the thunder rumbled like a distant cannonade, he swallowed, felt his hands sweating, and tried hard to fight down the fear that gripped him in the pit of his gut.

Chapter Six

As Ulysses, Sammy, and Mo sat together at lunch the next day at school, a group of five excited youths gathered around them. The cafeteria was a beehive of students.

"Hey, Man, is it true?" one of the boys asked, setting down his tray. "Did y'all whip the Cyclops?"

"We damn sure did!" Mo gave a fat-jawed grimace as he ate his sandwich.

"Damn, Man! How'd y'all do that?" another boy asked.

"We brass-knucked his ass!" Sammy said.

"Shit, I didn't believe nobody could whip that cave man!" another youth exclaimed.

The fourth boy boasted, "I would have fought his ass, too, if he had — "

Ulysses stopped eating and glared at him.

"Shit, you wouldn't have fought nobody, Sucker!" the first youth laughed. "Not with your scared ass! What y'all gonna do about the Philistines, Man?"

"Yeah, Man, them cats are bad. They bad to the bone marrow!" the fifth boy exclaimed. "I mean like they don't just rule the slums, they kill people, too! And shit, they into drugs, prostitution, extortion, and everything else they big enough to do. And they carry MAC-10s and Uzzis. I sure as hell wouldn't want to be on their hit list. Shit, I'd leave town!"

"Hell, anybody can get guns!" Sammy spat. "That ain't no big thing!"

As Ulysses ate nervously, another youth joined them. "Hey, Man, I heard the Cyclops was in the hospital. Man, you cats in a world of trouble. I hear that Dagon, who leads the Philistines — "

Ulysses jumped and shouted, "Shut up!"

They all jumped and looked at him, shocked.

"Sorry, Man, I didn't mean no harm," the boy apologized.

Ulysses sat back down. His appetite was gone, and he was shaking.

"Take it easy, Man," Sammy said.

Shaking their heads and mumbling to themselves, the boys made excuses and drifted off.

"How you feel, U?" Sammy asked.

"I'm okay."

"What y'all think, Man?" Mo swallowed, bugging his beady eyes.

Ulysses could hear the anxiety in Mo's voice, and he looked at his friends. He then sighed and shook his head. "I don't know."

"Well, Man, we knew what was gonna happen," Sammy said.

"Ain't happened yet," Mo uttered.

"Shit, but it's gonna happen. Y'all better get a gun, Man!" Sammy said. "'Cause I got one."

"That little .22 popgun?" Mo scoffed. "You better get a bigger one."

"I can't shoot nobody, Man," Ulysses shook his head and crumpled his milk carton.

"You better learn," Sammy uttered as the bell rang, ending lunch, and they got up to leave.

Chapter Seven

As Ulysses worked at the check-out counter after school that day at Acme Food Mart, the owner approached him.

"Got some bad news for you, Son."

"What's that, Mr. Rogers?" the youth asked, looking at the stout, dark-complected man.

"You'll probably have to start looking for another job by the end of the month. We're going out of business."

"What!" Ulysses was shocked. "You closing the store?"

"Don't want to. Got to."

"But why?"

"Look around you. Hardly any customers. Don't make enough no more, now that that big Safeway's moved in this area. I tried — cut my prices to the gristle, ran a bunch of special sales, gave folks credit, offered home delivery, you name it — didn't do no good. Just can't compete with no big chain outfit like that."

Ulysses shook his head and looked around the store. A few old women were shopping. "Yeah, I noticed that business has dropped off."

"Damn right it has. Lost most of my customers, too. Oh, don't get me wrong. I still have a few loyal ones, like your mother, who would trade with me no matter what because of the special service I offer and the line of goods I carry. But unfortunately, that's not enough." He stuck a toothpick in his mouth and chewed on it. "But, hell, Son, I don't blame folks. Times are hard, and they go where they can stretch their dollar the farthest and get what they want. Folks who never complained before say I'm high now. They just don't understand. . . ."

"Yeah, but some things they can't get at Safeway. Especially Black grooming products, and meats like mutton, neckbones, chitlings, pig feet —"

"Don't fool yourself, Boy. They'll be getting them there. Soon as customers start complaining and soon as the manager there finds out I carry them, they'll be getting them there. Anyway, you'll find something else, too."

"Yes, Sir," Ulysses shook his head as the owner walked off.

Chapter Eight

After work Ulysses got into his 1975 Ford Mustang and was about to pull out of the parking lot when another car pulled up and blocked him. The youth got out uneasily and faced four other men. They were dressed in fine double-breasted suits. One was Dagon, leader of the Philistines.

"What's happening, U?" he broke into a cold grin.

Ulysses shook his head. "Nothing much." He heard the anxiety in his own voice. Dagon unbuttoned his coat and put his hands on his hips, revealing the brown bone handle of a heavy-caliber magnum strapped to his chest in shoulder leather.

"Oh, now, that ain't so. There's a whole lot happening, My Man," Dagon said as his companions grinned. Ulysses saw the gun bulges in their coats, too.

Dagon stuck a cigarette in his mouth, and one of his boys fired it. Breaking into a cold sweat, Ulysses looked at the gunman, who appeared to be in his middle twenties, was brown-skinned, medium-built, and viper-eyed.

"We just finished powwowing with your friends Sammy and Mo." Dagon blew a stream of smoke from his nose. "We let them off the hook because they gonna perform a little service for us. And if they do it right, there may even be a little something in it for them."

The hoodlums looked at each other and chuckled.

Ulysses swallowed. "But not you, My Man!" Dagon dropped his cigarette and mashed it. Within a heartbeat, he drew his .357 Magnum, pointed it at Ulysses's head, and pulled the trigger. The hammer clicked, and the hoodlums roared as Dupree fell back against his car, threw up his hands, and hollered.

"You belong to the Cyclops," Dagon gnashed, putting the gun away. "But we know him as Arthur Lee, our chief enforcer. You see, we ain't killers like some people think. Are we, Boys?" The hoodlums shook their heads. "We businessmen. And when we have a problem with somebody, instead of shedding unnecessary blood, we simply turn the problem over to Arthur Lee. . . ." The hoods chuckled. "And then it just seems to disappear. Just like that!" he snapped his fingers. "Arthur Lee says ain't *nobody* to touch *you*. You special. He say he'll take care of you when he get on his feet."

Dagon grinned and lit another cigarette. "Now if I was you, you know what I'd do? *I'd* blow my own goddamn brains out now and make it easy on myself. Another thing. Don't leave town, Punk! You got that?" He shot a finger at Ulysses. "Otherwise, your mama and sister. . . . Know what I mean?" He then thumped his cigarette into Ulysses with a sneer. The hoods piled into their brand-new 1990 Mercedes and burned rubber out of the parking lot.

Bracing himself against his car, the youth wiped the cold sweat and took several deep breaths to calm himself. His mouth was cotton dry. Looking around numbly, he gazed at occasional traffic on Nineteenth Street. The surrounding small brick and frame houses now seemed very far away. When he brought his hand up to wipe his mouth, it was shaking badly.

"God!" he uttered, pulling himself together. He got into his car and drove home.

Chapter Nine

Monday and Tuesday of the following week were uneventful for Ulysses, but when he got home from work that Wednesday, his mother had some alarming news.

"Son," her face worked with anxiety, "I don't know how to tell you this."

"What is it?"

"Mo's dead."

"What!" Ulysses cried. "What are you talking about? I don't believe it! How? What happened?"

"The police shot him," Gwen said. "He and Sammy were burglarizing a store."

"Oh, Jesus!" Ulysses was numb. "I don't believe it!"

"Sammy's at home. He's out on bail. His mother called, and he wants to see you," Gwen said compassionately.

Tearing out of the house, Ulysses hurried to his car.

"Damn!" he cursed. It was sitting on a flat.

He took off down the street walking. Sammy lived six blocks away, and Ulysses hurried up and down several neighborhood streets of small run-down frame houses. The sky was overcast, and it started to sprinkle, then stopped. As trash blew in the gutters, the wind rose and came cold through the trees, carrying the fresh smell of wet earth and moldering leaves.

In a daze, Ulysses jumped when a big, black-and-white hound charged him from inside its chain-link fence. He frowned and cursed, then crossed the street and turned onto Twenty-third. Hurrying down the avenue in the cold, past rows of black businesses, he felt a heavy pain in his heart. Traffic was thick, and people moved up and down the boulevard going in and out of stores, shops, and restaurants.

When he passed a record store, he heard the heavy bass of rap music thumping inside. And as he hurried past a movie theater, he glanced at the show bill and saw that a gangster movie was playing.

"Say, U! Long time no see! What it look like, Homie? What it look like?" one of his classmates called, coming out of a barber shop.

"You got it, Dean! You got it!" he answered, looking at the tall, rawboned youth.

"Naw, Blood, it's your world! Say, Man, you think I got enough taken off the top?" He grinned, pointing at his skin head.

"Naw, Bro. You still look like an Old English sheepdog," Ulysses grinned.

Dean roared. "Be good, Homie. Be good." He said, slapping five with Dupree.

"You, too, Man, you, too!" Ulysses replied, hurrying on.

As he stood on the corner waiting for the light to change, an old man on a cane hobbled out of the Christ House Mission and left the door ajar. Ulysses could hear a priest inside, against the noisy traffic. "And the Lord said, 'I was hungry and you fed me, naked and you clothed me, sick and you cared for me, a stranger and you took me in. Because when you have done this for the least of my brethren, you have done it for me.' Remember, brothers and sisters, hunger knows no race, sickness knows no sex, nakedness knows no age. . . ."

Glancing back into the mission and seeing a number of homeless people, both black and white, sitting at tables eating and listening, the youth hurried on.

When he got to Sammy's house in a dilapidated neighborhood on Twenty-sixth, Sammy's mother opened the door. Ulysses gazed at the tall, dark-complected, thin woman. Her eyes were puffy and red.

"Come in, U," she uttered, grief-stricken.

"Mrs. Aaron, I'm so sorry."

She shook her head as three little children sat watching cartoons on television in the small, run-down house.

"U, why?" She wiped her eyes. "Why my boy want to throw his life away like that? You his friend. Maybe you know." She dropped her head and shook it.

"No, Ma'am," he swallowed. "I don't know. Where's Sammy?"

"He out back."

"Can I go and see him?"

"Yeah. He want to see you."

As Ulysses hurried through the house, he noticed that the children were watching "Cinderella" on television. When he got outside, he saw Sammy standing at the end of the crabgrassy backyard, gazing up the alley that ran behind the house. Ulysses pulled up his coat collar against the cold, gray evening. When Sammy turned, they embraced.

"Oh, Man! Oh, Man!" Sammy sobbed, and they were both sobbing now. Ulysses felt his friend shaking. "Mo's gone, Man! He's gone!" Sammy wept. "We can't bring him back. He's gone forever! Oh, God! Oh, God!"

"It's my fault, Man!" Ulysses grieved. "It's my fault. Y'all were just helping me out, Man! Now, look what I done caused."

"Naw, Man, don't blame yourself. You'd have done the

same thing for us. We all *Homies,* Man. All for one. Remember? That's what real friendship is all about anyway — suffering and dying for each other."

"I know, I know. You think the Philistines set you up, Man?"

"I don't know. Don't much matter now."

"No."

"I go to trial in a couple of weeks," Sammy said, pulling himself together and wiping his eyes.

"What you think you'll get?"

"I don't know. My first offense. Maybe the judge, he go easy on me."

"Yeah," Ulysses sighed. "I hope so."

"When I get out, though," Sammy looked off at the windblown trees, scattering leaves, "football's over for me, Man. Maybe my life, too. I don't know.

"Oh, no, Man. You young."

"Yeah, but that place make you old. And you an ex-con after that." Sammy peered up at the dreary, gray sky and moved in place to keep warm. His breath fluttered white in the wind. "They gonna send me to MacAlester. I'll get at least five years, I know. Black man ain't got no chance in this system. You know that. Especially if he's poor. White man against us, our own *people* against us. Shit, prison mostly full of brothers, anyway. That ain't no accident." Sammy scuffed his shoe in the dirt. "But why our own people got to be against us, U? Why our own *people* got to be against us?" Sammy clenched his teeth and made a fist.

Ulysses dropped his head and shook it. He didn't have an answer.

Suddenly they heard a choir of honking overhead, and when they looked up, a small formation of wild geese were flying over, fairly low. Ulysses watched them ride the cold, wet air, moving with a smooth, powerful grace.

"Wherever they going," Sammy yearned, "I'd give anything to be going with them."

Ulysses looked at his friend as Sammy's eyes grew misty and forlorn.

"Yeah," Dupree sighed.

"Anyway," Sammy wiped his eyes as the birds receded into the distant pearl-gray sky, "listen, Man, don't tell my mama nothing. Philistines say if she makes trouble, they gonna fix her, and my little brothers, too."

Ulysses shook his head.

"What you gonna do, Man?" Sammy asked. "They saving you for the Cyclops. But you can't leave town, I know."

"I don't know, Blood, what I'm gonna do," Ulysses sweated in the cold. "I should get me a gun, but. . . ." He dropped his head and shook it. "I ain't no killer."

"Yeah, well, good luck to you, Bro. And God protect you!" Sammy extended his hand, and his friend shook it.

"Good luck to you, too, Homie. And God be with you. I'll come by and see you again before. . . ."

"Okay."

They embraced again, and Dupree turned and trudged off.

Chapter Ten

When Ulysses got home, he fixed his flat and sat down to dinner with his sister and mother.

"Mama, I ain't got much of an appetite," he said.

"Well, try to eat a little something, anyway," she replied, helping his plate. "So what's the story, Son?"

He told her.

"Sammy couldn't understand why our own people got to be against us, Mama. And neither can I." Ulysses dropped his head and shook it.

"Don't suspect nobody really knows the answer to that, Son. Just the way it's always been. I suspect it's part of the defect in man's nature. Don't forget *The Bible* tells us it was Jesus's own people who demanded his death. And Joseph's own brothers wanted to kill him, but later sold him into slavery, just like our own African ancestors did their own. But you still got to help your people, Son. 'Cause there are still an awful lot of good ones. No matter what, you can't give up on them." Mrs. Dupree looked at Gwen. "Jesus and Joseph showed us that. You just can't deny your people."

"Yes, Ma'am," Ulysses replied.

"I feel so bad," Gwen wiped the tears. "All of this happened because Mo and Sammy were trying to help me, just like always."

"Okay, now you and Gwen got to leave here. I'm sending her to Tulsa to her Aunt Mandy's, and Dr. Johnson say you can go to stay with his sister in Guthrie." Mrs. Dupree looked at her son.

"What about you, Mama?" he exclaimed.

"Yeah!" Gwen uttered. "You're gonna be in danger if you stay here."

"Naw, I'll be all right."

"Ain't no way I'm running off and leaving you here," Ulysses said.

"Now, listen," his mother replied. "Dr. Johnson said his friend's a policeman, and he'll look after me if we do this."

"How's he gonna protect you?" her son cried. "It can't be done. If the Philistines want you, can't nobody protect you."

"Maybe not. But the doctor say his friend *and* the Chief of Police gonna talk to these boys. Gonna tell them if anything happen to me, they gonna know who to come for, and they gonna come down on them with everything they got."

"Aw, Mama, I don't know . . ." Ulysses shook his head.

"Son, that's all we got. And as far as I'm concerned, it's enough. Anyway, that's the way it's gonna be, 'cause y'all going, and I'm staying, and that's that. So let's eat."

Ulysses looked at his sister, sighed, and shook his head again.

"I said let's eat!" their mother demanded.

The teenagers began pecking at their food.

They all ate silently and thoughtfully. Toward the end of dinner, Ulysses said, "That doctor's sure swell, ain't he?"

"Ain't many like him," his mother replied. "We privileged to know him and blessed to have him for a friend." She looked off thoughtfully. "Sometimes one man can make a difference where it counts and where it's sorely needed —

among his own. Always remember that, Son."

"I will, Mama. I will."

"Folks say everything in the ghetto is ugly. But sometimes you find a wild rose growing straight up through the concrete."

"Yes, Ma'am." Ulysses looked at his mother and nodded his head.

CHAPTER ELEVEN

The next day Ulysses and Gwen decided to have lunch together. He waited for her beside his car in the school parking lot. It was a rainy, overcast day. Presently he saw her coming, carrying her folded umbrella in one hand and purse over the other shoulder. She looked dapper in her red rain coat, and moved with a light, swinging grace. A few students and teachers came and went in their cars.

"Let's walk, U," she said.

"It's raining."

"No, it's not," she held out her palm and smiled.

"What if it starts?"

"Come on, you lazy bum. I've got my umbrella." Locking her arm through his, she started him out of the parking lot. They proceeded down the street.

"How's it going?" he asked.

"Okay. Not as bad as I thought."

"Good."

"U, I want to talk to you seriously."

"Okay," he replied, watching cars hiss by on the wet pavement and glancing at the run-down houses and apartments that surrounded the school.

"Listen, Honey, you've got a wonderful opportunity

before you. Do you know that?" she asked.

"What do you mean?"

"Well, you're going to stay with Dr. Johnson's sister, and she's got money and no kids."

"So?"

"Don't you see? If you please her, she could be your benefactress to college."

"Now, wait a minute —"

"No, now listen to me," she held up her hand. "Dr. Johnson said she's all alone, except for her niece who's away in college. And she's always wanted a son, but never had one. Don't you see? This could be your big opportunity. You could be that son. It's possible. If you play your cards well and she takes a fancy to you, she could make your future. I mean it. It can happen."

"Whoa! whoa! whoa! Slow down, Sugar. You're going way too fast." Ulysses laughed. "You're in storybook land. You know that?"

"I'm not!" she cried. "Why does that sound so preposterous to you?"

"If you think I'm gonna suck up to a wealthy old woman so she'll be my fairy godmother —"

"I didn't mean *that,* Ulysses!" she exclaimed. "She could see through that in a minute."

"Then what?" he smiled with amusement.

It started to sprinkle, and Gwen popped her umbrella open and handed it to her brother. "Just be yourself — your nice, decent, well-raised, hard-working self. The young man that Mama reared."

"Yeah, sure," he rolled his eyes as they turned onto the busy boulevard of fast-food restaurants.

"U, I didn't say that she *would* take a fancy to you, but that she might. Now, I want to talk about what happens if she *does,*" Gwen enthused.

"But why would she?" he asked. "There are plenty of fine young men in Guthrie she could take a fancy to and make their future, if she wanted to. Why she waiting for me?"

"U, in a lot of ways you're smart, but in a lot of ways, you're not."

"What you mean?"

"You have to have an opportunity to be close to people, one-on-one, for a period of time before a real attachment forms. And you're probably the only boy who has ever gotten this opportunity. Don't you see? Doesn't that make sense?"

He gazed soberly into his sister's beautiful brown eyes for a moment. Then he glanced at the busy and noisy traffic splashing by in the rain.

"U, an education is the most important thing in the world for poor people, but especially minorities."

"I know," he sighed.

"Without it, we might as well be dead, because we have no future. If we cannot individually, through education, lift ourselves out of the slums, we will waste away here. You know that, too! Everything we want — a nice home, spouse, children, job, financial security, social standing — everything we want lies *outside* the ghetto. That's why we have to make good any opportunity to acquire a higher education or a vocational skill."

"What about Dr. Johnson?"

"He's *got* an education, U. Who's to say how long he's gonna give to his missionary work in the slums? Just give yourself the same chance."

He chuckled. "I want to go to college. You talk like I don't want to."

"Yes, but you don't want it bad enough, I think. I don't really think you see the full significance —"

"Why don't I?" he cried.

"Because if you did, you'd hitch your wagon to a star. You'd make better grades and try to polish up your English, for one thing."

He sighed. "I guess I just never really thought I could ever go to college or trade school. What you want to eat?"

"I don't know. Something light, nothing fattening."

"A salad?"

"That sounds good."

"We can get one in here." He nodded at the pizza place they were now in front of.

She took hold of his arm and stopped him.

"Do you see what I'm trying to say? I won't wind up like Mama. I swear it."

"Mama's a good woman."

"I know that!" Gwen exclaimed. "Morally she's the best, but professionally — cooking and cleaning for other people. . . . You know what I mean. . . ."

"Yeah, I understand."

"Do you really?"

"Sure. Why not?"

"Then promise me one thing."

"All right," he sighed.

"Don't throw your life away. Don't end up like Sammy or Mo or like those older men we see — down and out with nothing but a house full of kids they can't or won't half provide for." The wind blew tendrils of hair in her face, and she brushed them away thoughtfully. "Fine, eligible, young black men are in such short supply these days. Because Black men are so busy hurting one another, committing crimes, and going to jail. Now, you've got a wonderful opportunity before you, Honey. Just make the most of it. Okay? For God's sake, wake up and smell the coffee, will you?"

Listening to the noisy traffic, Ulysses nosed the cool, rainy air. "I don't smell no coffee. I thought you said you wanted salad?"

Perturbed, she sighed, shook her head, and looked at him.

"You're sure cute when you get mad," he teased. "Boy, if Mama and Dr. Johnson could have heard *that* pep talk. . . ."

"Come on!" she grabbed his arm, walking him inside. "You make me sick!"

He grinned.

Chapter Twelve

On Friday Ulysses and his family attended Mo's funeral. It was a heart-rending service that Ulysses and Sammy took as hard as the immediate family did. A lot of Mo's relatives and classmates also attended. When the service was over, both youths expressed their heart-felt condolences to Mo's mother and kid brother. Ulysses then had an emotional and misty-eyed parting with Sammy, and they promised to stay in touch always and reunite as soon as Sammy was out of prison.

Having quit his job, Ulysses packed up his bags that Saturday evening. After saying good-bye to his mother and sister, he followed Dr. Johnson to his sister's home in Guthrie and embarked upon a new stage in his life.

Lying some thirty-five miles north of Oklahoma City, Guthrie was a fine old country town that had once been the state capital. When the two men got to their destination, they pulled into the driveway of a grand old white two-story house in a neighborhood of elegant, old, terraced Victorian homes. Turning up his jacket collar against the dreary cold and the overcast sky, the youth looked around and smiled as snow flurries danced through the air. It was sure going to be swell living in a town such as this, he thought, away from the crime and violence of the city. It would truly be a new lease on life.

The doctor helped him carry his bags up to the porch, and then rang the doorbell. A short, plump, elderly woman who looked to be in her late sixties opened the door and broke into a handsome smile.

"Sis, this is Ulysses Dupree. U, this is my sister, Mrs. Edna Mae Hatcher."

"Pleased to meet you, Ma'am," Ulysses smiled.

"The pleasure is all mine," she beamed. "He's a fine-looking boy," she said to her brother. "Y'all come on in." She held the door open. "Just put the bags down anywhere for now."

The house, grand and elegant, was full of well-dressed people who were leaving. There were two black men, a white man, and a black woman.

"Thanks again for your support, Mae," the tall heavy-set, dignified-looking gentleman said, getting into his over-coat. He was brown-skinned, with gray-streaked hair, and he wore a fine gray suit.

"That's quite all right, Senator," she smiled as they hugged. "Oh, you all know my brother, Dr. Robert Johnson?"

"Oh, yes. How are you, Bob?"

"Just fine, Sir. And you?"

"Never better. Never better," the senator boomed. "You know my staff — Dave, Bill, and Nancy?"

"Oh, yes. Of course. How are you all?"

They smiled, shook hands, and spoke.

"This is Ulysses Dupree," the doctor introduced. "U, this is Senator John Douglass."

"How are you, young man?"

"Just fine, Sir. And you?" Ulysses asked, watching his English and smiling at the politician, who appeared to be in his late fifties.

"Fine! Fine!" He shook hands. "How old are you, Son?"

"Seventeen."

"Not quite old enough to vote yet, huh?"

"No, Sir."

They all chuckled.

"Well, I hope to see you again, then — to acquaint you with our political views, so that in the next election, we might have your support, too, if you like what we stand for."

"All right," Ulysses smiled.

"And, Bob, I'd sure appreciate your support in the next election, too."

"You've got it, as usual, Senator."

"Mighty fine! Mighty fine! Well, we'll say good-night then."

"Good-night, Sir," Mae said, as he and his staff left.

"He's a good man," she uttered, shutting the door. "He fights hard for our people."

"Yes, he does," her brother agreed.

"So this is Ulysses Dupree, huh?" she asked.

"Uh-huh," her brother replied, as Ulysses smiled.

"A fine-looking boy. Sit down, everybody. Sit down!" Mae offered.

As he did so, Ulysses looked around the house. It had a fresh, pleasant smell and was cozy and warm against the dreary cold. He glanced at the large, roaring fireplace, the elegant furnishings, and the fine grand piano that stood in a glass-enclosed music room off of the dining room. The house was also done in beautiful maroon and green French Provincial decor. It rather took the youth's breath away to know that he would live in a place such as this.

Chapter Thirteen

The doctor had to leave before long, but before doing so he helped Ulysses carry his bags up to his room, which was very nice and comfortable. Ulysses then walked him out to his car. It was cold and snowing.

"Thanks for giving me a leg up, Doc — for being my mentor and looking after my home while I'm away."

"My pleasure, Son. And don't worry about a thing. I'm sure it's all gonna work out."

"I hope so," Ulysses smiled, and they embraced.

"I'd better be going. I want to beat this weather in." The doctor looked up at the big flakes coming down.

"All right," Ulysses said and watched him get in his car and drive off. They waved.

The youth then looked at the snow swirling and falling, up and down the fine old neighborhood street. Filling his lungs with the cold, clean air, he rushed back inside.

Ulysses and Mrs. Hatcher had coffee in her kitchen, which was beautiful and spacious, with knotty-pine cabinets and fine large appliances. The room was also done in a very cheerful yellow and white color scheme and had a fine, clean smell.

"Would you like something to eat, Ulysses?"

"No, thank you. I just ate before coming over. But

please call me 'U.' Everybody does."

"All right," she smiled. "You may call me 'Mae.' Everybody does."

"All right," he chuckled, looking into her pleasant, light, brown-complected face. She wore gold earrings and her hair was pulled back in a bun.

"So you want to finish up your senior year here, huh?"

"Yes. And I'd like to get an after-school job to help pay my room and board with you."

"I like that. That shows character. I'll make a few phone calls. Then what?"

"What do you mean?" he asked, trying to speak correctly and looking into her shrewd, searching eyes.

"I mean what after high school?"

"Well," he thought, "I'll go to work full-time then, and get my own place, and maybe one day I can save enough to go to college."

"You never will," she threw cold water on the idea and startled him.

"What do you mean?"

"What do you know how to do?"

"Nothing, really."

"Then you'll take an unskilled job at minimum wage?"

"Yes."

"Well, once you pay your living and recreational expenses, you'll never be able to put aside enough to go to school."

"I see."

"Of course, you can get loans and work while going to college, but that would be a struggle, and you'd have little or no social life. So school would be an uphill battle all the way. And even after you graduated, you'd have a big debt hanging over you."

"Yes," he said thoughtfully.

"Of course, there's also trade school, which wouldn't take as long, but would present the same drawbacks and the degree would be much more limiting."

"Yes, Ma'am."

"If you did go to college, any idea what you'd major in?"

"Well, my best grades are in math. . . ."

"What math have you had?"

"I'm taking trig now."

"Good. Math is a good major," she said, sipping her coffee. "Always in demand and pays well. Money is very important, you know."

"Yes, ma'am."

"I've pursued it all my life. That's why I have this home, a fine restaurant downtown, interest in a number of other businesses, money in the bank, rental property, and oil- and gas-bearing land. I have also flown to Alaska and Japan on vacation and taken luxury cruises to Europe, Hawaii, the Virgin Islands, and the Bahamas. And I started out with nothing but a college degree that my parents struggled to enable me to acquire." She smiled pleasantly.

"That's amazing!"

"Perhaps. But it's more a matter of wanting a thing more than anything else in the world and going after it in a hard and single-minded way. And, of course, being much blessed by God in the process. If you don't have money in this country, you're nothing. You get sick, you can't afford to go to the doctor, and if you die, you can't bury yourself. You believe that?"

"Oh, yes, Ma'am," he said, admiring her. "Money is the most important thing in this country. But. . . ."

"But what?"

"What about Dr. Johnson's belief?"

"To be perfectly honest with you, Young Man, my brother's a wonderful man, but I've never understood him."

"What do you mean?"

"I guess you'd call him an idealist living in a material country. It's hard to prosper when you're out of sync like that. Know what I mean?"

"I think so," he replied, glancing out into the beautiful backyard, at the chilly, gray sky and trees and lawn, powdered with snow.

"My brother is the most brilliant man I know. He has more education than any man I know. He's pursued it all of his life. And acquired it not only through working hard at part-time jobs, but also through scholarships, fellowships, and grants because of his great intellect."

She got up to get another cup of coffee. "And he could be rich by now — or darn near it, if he wanted to. Yet he chooses not to be. Why? because he prefers to be a barefoot jungle doctor — an Albert Schweitzer type." Mae chuckled and shook her head. "Even when we were kids, he was that way. Always helping people and expecting nothing in return. And make no mistake — a lot of folks used him, too. But, you know, if his own health failed him today, I'd have to go in and find him, bring him out, and take care of him — which I wouldn't mind, you understand. But, Son, it's one thing to dedicate yourself to a cause, and quite another to have nothing to show for it in the end. Even preachers are supported by the church. And the big-shot ones have big cars and big bank accounts to prove it."

"Yes, Ma'am," he said thoughtfully.

"This is a capitalistic country, Son. Built and run on money." She sat back down. "I don't care what anybody says. Look around you. All the big business that operates this nation is profit-driven. Everything that is not cost-effective is cut. Now, that's reality. Anything else is fantasy."

"I see," he said excitedly, drinking in her philosophy because she was living proof of its soundness. There was also an air of importance about her, and he had never heard anyone speak this way before who could lift the curtain on the power behind the throne of success.

"Now, don't get me wrong." She held up a finger. "I ain't preaching the gospel of pure materialism. Because there's more to life than money. Money is not a cure-all for all of life's problems. You've got to have God, too, because you can't take any of this with you when you die. But you can do even more for God when you have money. I give a lot to the church, to colleges, to charity, and to various worthwhile causes, not to mention political campaigns, like that of Senator Douglass."

He smiled admiringly and sipped his coffee.

"I also have no shortage of friends."

"You're not married?" he asked, encouraged by her openness and good nature.

"My husband was killed in World War II, and I never remarried."

"I see. What about relatives?"

"Only Dr. Johnson and Cynthia, who is his only child by a former marriage. She's a little older than you, and a freshman at Oklahoma State University."

"Dr. Johnson's not married now?"

"No."

"I see."

"You want some more coffee?"

"No," he smiled. "I'm fine."

She looked off thoughtfully. "That's funny. I've never talked like this to anybody before and can't imagine why I'm doing it now." She looked down and circled the rim of her cup with her ring finger. Ulysses noticed the large diamond ring. "Cynthia's like my daughter. We're very close. I practically raised her after her mother passed. She's closer to me than she is to her own father, and I've put everything into her that I know. She's something. You'll see. It's just that — well, sometimes things don't pan out. I made a lot of mistakes with her. Broke most of my own rules. I'll be the first to admit that. You know, Son, sometimes we think we know what we want until we get it. . . ." Mrs. Hatcher frowned and sighed. "It was a wise man who said, 'There are two things to aim at in life: First, to get what you want; and after that, to enjoy it. Only the wisest of mankind achieve the second.' Anyway, now that I'm getting on in years, I find that my happiness is not complete after all. . . ."

"What would complete it?"

She looked up and smiled. "That, young Ulysses Dupree, is an old woman's secret that I may or may not get around to telling you."

"All right," he chuckled.

"You know, my brother and I disagree a lot, but we are in agreement on one thing — the importance of hard work, education, and self-reliance."

"I believe that, too. With all my heart!"

"Yes, I believe you do." She searched his face, gripped his hand, then slapped her legs and rose.

He rose, too.

"Oh, before I forget it. Do you smoke or drink?"

"I smoke on occasion, but I don't drink. I never have."

"Good. We'll get along. Come on. I want to show you around town before it's dark. Looks like the snow has stopped for now. Move your car out of the way, and we'll take mine. I just bought it and haven't had a chance to break it in yet."

"What kind is it?"

"A Cadillac."

He smiled.

Chapter Fourteen

The next day Ulysses enrolled in Guthrie High School and began attending classes. He got the same courses that he had had in Oklahoma City, and the teachers were about at the same point in their instruction. Mrs. Hatcher got him a part-time job at Ken's Barbecue Pit, since she had no openings in her restaurant.

The first Saturday in November, Ulysses went to get a haircut at Ed's Barber Shop in the Black part of town. It was a small, drab-looking shop, and a middle-aged minister waited his turn.

"Ain't seen you here before, Son," Ed said.

"No, I just moved here."

"Where you from?"

"Oklahoma City."

"I see. You got people here, do you?" The old man used his clippers.

"No, but I'm staying with Mrs. Hatcher."

"Edna Mae?"

"Yes, Sir."

"That's *nice!* You must be somebody special." He looked at the boy.

"Oh, no, Sir. She's just a very kind lady."

"Yeah, and a rich one, too."

The minister and the old man chuckled.

"Yes, she's about the richest Black person in Guthrie. No telling how much she's worth," the minister tossed off.

"Ain't no question about that," Ed agreed.

Ulysses smiled at the wiry, gray-headed old haircutter, who, like many in his profession, was a gossip.

"She don't belong to my church," the minister declared. "Don't even belong to my faith, but every Christmas she gives us a handsome donation to help the needy."

"That's wonderful!" Ed exclaimed. "Just wonderful!"

"Sure is!" the preacher replied. "It surely is."

Ed continued talking as he worked. "You going to high school or college?"

"I'm finishing my senior year in high school."

"Then I suspect you'll be going to college, huh?"

"I hope so."

"Well, if Edna Mae likes you, you got it made, Son."

The minister looked up from his magazine and shook his head.

"Especially because she ain't never had no one living with her before, that I know of — except that pretty niece of hers. Son, you mighty lucky, you know that?" Ed asked.

"The Lord's blessed him dearly," the minister put in. "Just always carry God with you, Young Man, and don't ever turn your back on your people, and God will heap blessings on you a hundredfold."

"Amen, Pastor!" the barber exclaimed, nudging Ulysses, who smiled.

"Why do you think God blessed Moses the way He did?" the pastor said. "Because Moses put his people before himself."

"Say it, Pastor! Say it!" Ed crowed.

Ulysses smiled, then looked out into the afternoon cold. Traffic streamed past the dismal-looking businesses across the street. One young woman was going into the beauty shop, and a middle-aged man was coming out of the cleaners, carrying a suit. Up the street, Ulysses could see a busy service station.

"Yeah, I been cutting hair here for nigh on thirty years," Ed informed.

"Is that right?"

"That's right. And I done seen it all. I suspect I'll get to cut your hair for a few more years. 'Cause if you around here or at the university, ain't nowhere else you can go and get a first-rate haircut."

"I see."

"Yeah. I see all the men hereabout at one time or another. Of course, the college boys graduate and move on, though."

"They don't stay, huh?"

"Nah, they don't see that there's anything for them here, but they wrong. We got over ten thousand people in this town."

"I see," Ulysses smiled with amusement.

"Yeah, but folks see what they want to see," the minister spoke up. "Young folks don't want to see. That's the problem. All they interested in is sex, drugs, loud music, and cars. They sure don't come to church, especially the educated ones. I don't know what the country's coming to."

"You right about that, Pastor," the barber agreed.

Oh, boy! Ulysses sighed and rolled his eyes.

"Yeah, they think we ain't got nothing for them," the preacher went on. "But God's got a heap for them, and they sure as heck need it."

Clearing his throat, Ed used his scissors. "I suspect the college kids go to the chapel on the campus, though."

"Yeah, but they need to mingle with black folks in the community so that these young folks don't ever forget their culture and heritage," the pastor replied. "They need to use their education to help the church reach out to its people through its social, educational, and religious programs in the community. That's why God's blessed them in the first place — as a means to help uplift their people. But," he sighed, "most young, educated black folks and older, successful ones don't see it that way at all. They don't see that they got a moral obligation whatsoever. They don't seem to realize who made it possible for them to get where they are. So many of them are scornful of their roots, anyway, and think they above the Black community. But they as wrong as they can be. They done forgot the teachings of Booker T. Washington and Dr. Dubois, — that is, if they ever knew them."

As the Reverend dropped his head and shook it, Ulysses hoped that meant that he had gotten his grievances out of his system and perhaps talked himself out.

"You right about that, Reverend Drew." The old man rubbed his bald spot thoughtfully. "My place and the beauty parlor across the street is about the only ones the college kids go to in the Black community any more. And they wouldn't come here if they didn't have to."

Yeah, because you'd talk them to death instead of cut their hair, Ulysses sighed heavily, feeling like a scapegoat.

"Sure." The minister put down his magazine and looked up with renewed vigor, obviously having gotten his second wind.

Damn! Ulysses spat.

"Once Black folks get a little education and money," the Reverend went on, "they move out away from their own, into the white community, and start patronizing white businesses and trying to hobnob with white folks. They don't stick together. They too busy trying to cut one another down, and the successful ones are all for self and done forgot their own."

Ulysses shifted his weight and grew impatient for the

old man to finish. The minister was starting to repeat himself. And this gripe session, which the youth felt was put on, for his benefit, had slowed the barber down to a crawl.

"Oh, yeah!" Ed hawked and spat tobacco juice into a spittoon as he combed the youth's hair back with a pick. "If we don't help each other, ain't nobody else gonna do it! And that's the truth!"

"Do you have a church home here, Son?" the preacher asked.

"No, Sir." Ulysses started to freeze because he knew what was coming.

"What church did you attend in the city, if I may ask?"

He wanted to say *What the hell business is it of yours?* But instead, stammered, "Well, I, — I — ."

"You didn't have a church home. Is that it? I understand. I understand perfectly. You see, Brother Brown," the pastor declared, wavering on the threshold of his pulpit voice, "one of the main problems is that the youth of today do not have their faith anchored in the Holy Spirit through the Black church. Which historically has been our strength and salvation." Trying to hide his resentment and keep his cool, Ulysses gazed at the Reverend, who was a small, spare, pop-eyed man and who peered out judgmentally over horn-rimmed glasses. "Therefore, they forget how God has protected and blessed them through the sacrifice and suffering of the old ones. You see, it was the old ones who formed the bridge that. . . ."

The youth stopped listening as the barber turned him in the chair so he could inspect himself in the mirror. He wanted a bit more taken off the sides, but instead he paid the old man, took off the chair cloth, got up, and left, even before the barber could brush him off.

"Hurry back, Son!" the old-timer hollered.

"Like hell I will!" he snarled and took a deep breath as

he stepped out into the cool, fresh air. "Hell, all I wanted was a damn haircut, not a long-ass sermon!" He then got into his Mustang and fired up a cigarette. Throwing the car in gear, he burned rubber away from the curb.

CHAPTER FIFTEEN

Ulysses's life passed smoothly during the following weeks. He made a few friends at school and continued his part-time job. At times, working after school and getting his homework done were hard. But he determined to make the most of his opportunities and make a success of his life. By now he and Mae had also struck up a warm and close relationship.

For Thanksgiving, his mother went to Tulsa to be with his sister and aunt, and he, Mae, and Dr. Johnson enjoyed a nice Thanksgiving dinner together. Cynthia, whom he was yet to meet, spent the holiday with her boyfriend.

Ulysses talked with his mother often by phone, and on Sunday drove to the city to spend the day with her. Parking in the alley behind the house, he did not have any trouble, nor had the Philistines tried to bother his mother in any way.

As Christmas approached, Mae's home was decorated beautifully for the season. And a big, lovely Christmas tree with lots of presents under it glittered in the big picture window of the living room. But it was the first Saturday in December that the youth would never forget, because that was when Cynthia came home to visit.

Mae was excitedly preparing breakfast, and Ulysses and Dr. Johnson sat in the front room talking. When the new yellow Camaro pulled up in front of the house, Ulysses's heart fluttered, and Dr. Johnson called to Mae.

"She's here!"

"All right!" Mae answered and came bustling into the frontroom. But as Cynthia got out of her car, a beautiful, metallic-gold Firebird pulled up behind her, and Ulysses noticed that Mae's face fell. Dr. Johnson also dropped his head and shook it as they all stood in the doorway. Cynthia's boyfriend then swaggered over and put his arm around her.

As Ulysses watched them come up the steps, he felt a surge of excitement that took his breath away because he had never seen a more gorgeous or voluptuous young lady. She was about five-feet nine and very fair, with long, black, silky, curly hair that bounced over her slim shoulders. Moving with the easy grace of a Greek goddess, she wore a green brooched choker and smart green high heels that matched her elegant, short, tight, green dress suit. And the suit molded to her fashion-model figure and showed off her beautiful curves and shapely legs.

But when Ulysses focused on the young man beside her, he could understand the disappointment of her relatives. The fellow was a brute, a dark-complected, crudely handsome, powerfully built football player for the 0.S.U. Cowboys. His presence was awe-inspiring, Ulysses thought, for he must have been six-feet four and weighed at least two hundred forty pounds. His jeans fit snugly around his narrow waist and big thighs, and his shoulder span, in his athletic windbreaker, was awesome.

When she breezed in and her boyfriend boomed in behind her, Cynthia threw herself into her aunt's arms with kisses and words of endearment. The gridder roared, "What it look like, Doc?"

"How are you doing, James?" Dr. Johnson replied and flinched from the power of the vice that gripped his hand.

"Don't break my hand, Son. I have to practice medicine."

James roared, "Sorry about that, Doc. But I always feel good when I'm out with my little filly!"

"This is Ulysses Dupree, a friend of the family," the doctor introduced. "U, this is James Babbitt."

"How are you doing, Sonny?" he grabbed Ulysses's hand, gripping it equally hard as he stared down through primitive eyes. Ulysses returned a firm grasp, and the two men stared each other down.

"It's 'Ulysses,' not 'Sonny,'" the youth corrected.

Releasing his hand with a slight shove, the gridder's face hardened in a slow burn.

After Cynthia and her father had hugged and kissed, Mae said, "Ulysses, this is Cynthia."

"I'm so happy to meet you," he smiled, his heart taking wing as he touched her hand. "I've heard so much about you."

"And I you," she smiled. "It's a great pleasure." Her voice rang with mirth and music.

The youth felt chills go up and down his body as they looked deep into each other's eyes, and she embraced him in the warmth of her stare, casting a spell on him. For a moment, they were the only two people in the room.

James cleared his throat disapprovingly.

"I understand you're a senior this year in high school?" she queried.

"Yes," he replied, watching his English.

"Well, I hope you'll come to O.S.U. next year."

"That would be nice," he answered, looking at her beautiful, creamy complexion, her full sensual lips traced in pastel pink, and her lovely, dark, Circean eyes.

"It sure would," she smiled, as her honeyed voice continued to caress him.

"Yeah!" James blared. "Then you get to see *me* play!"

He jabbed a thumb at himself.

"Yes!" Cynthia exclaimed. "James is the star quarterback for the Cowboys. He's *really* something! You should see him in action. They say he's Heisman material!"

"Yeah, and we going all the way this year! Number one!" James shot out a finger and grinned.

"What kind of season are you all having so far?" the doctor asked.

"Are you kidding? Ain't you been keeping up? Shit, we kicking ass!" James boomed. "Gonna stomp O.U. in the ground, too, this year!"

Ulysses noticed that Cynthia flattened her hand on her ample breast, and lit up over him as though he were a Greek Olympian. It was sickening, the youth thought.

"The pros are really after him, too, Daddy!" she uttered. "And he's only in his second year. And gosh! As you can well imagine, every girl on campus wants him. But I'm the lucky one." She locked her arm though his.

That's a matter of opinion, Ulysses thought, and rolled his eyes.

"And, Auntie, there's no telling how much *money* he's gonna make. Way up into the eight figures, I know. Isn't that exciting?" she caught her breath, gazing up at him with worshipful eyes, as though he were a golden calf.

Mae sighed and forced a smile as James stuck out his chest and assumed an air of almighty self-importance.

"Let's hope he doesn't get hurt," Ulysses said.

"What you talking about? I ain't gonna get hurt!" James barked. "Ain't nobody gonna hurt *me!* Yeah, we gonna have a big house, too, Baby! Finer than this one! Out in Quail Creek among the rich white dogs. And I'm gonna play golf at the country club. And we gonna have two Cadillacs and two Mercedes," he grinned primitively at Cynthia. "And you ain't gonna have nothing to do, but stay looking cute, Sugar." He plucked her cheek.

"Oh, my! That's the American dream!" she blushed.

"Yeah, sure," Mae said flatly as Doctor Johnson gave a painful smile. "Ulysses, Dear, would you go to the store for me? I'm kind of low on sugar."

"Be glad to."

"Hey, Mae!" James roared. "How you been, Old Gal?"

"Just fine, Son. Just fine," she replied, swallowing her disgust. "Well, everybody, sit down. Breakfast in a bit."

"Let's dig some football on the tube!" James boomed.

Ulysses went upstairs to get his jacket, and when he came down, James and Cynthia were sitting close together on the couch, watching the game. Ulysses smiled at her, and she smiled back. But when he stepped out onto the porch, James came out behind him.

"Say, Joker!" he snarled. "Lighten up on my woman. You got that?" He poked Ulysses in the chest with his finger.

"What you talking about?"

"You know what I mean! Don't play dumb with me! I don't like the way you coming on to her!"

"Shit, Man, you crazy!" Ulysses said, then turned and walked off. James then came after him, grabbed him by the shoulder, and snatched him around. Both men balled up their fists, squared off, and glared at each other. Ulysses backed off and ran his errand.

Chapter Sixteen

When he got back, Ulysses sat down in the front room with the others. Mae was in the kitchen finalizing breakfast. The youth was nervous and lit a cigarette. As he and Dr. Johnson talked, he felt torn between not wanting any trouble with James, on the one hand, but on the other hand being unable to keep his eyes off of Cynthia. When he looked at her, she set him on fire and held him spellbound, and he could not look away. The cigarette did, however, calm him a bit and steady his nerves.

"Man, don't you know those coffin nails ain't good for you?" James frowned when a commercial came on TV.

Ulysses smiled. "Well, it's nice to know that you care, Homie."

James sneered.

"As a physician, I suppose I should be the first to tell you that," Dr. Johnson grinned.

Ulysses shrugged. "I only smoke occasionally, Doc."

In spite of himself, his eyes were drawn back to Cynthia.

She was staring at him, and he stared back.

James noticed it again, and his face hardened and his jaws tightened.

"How's school, Honey?" Dr. Johnson asked his daughter.

"Just fine, Daddy."

"Good! You ever thought about playing for a Black school, James? Like Dubois University here in Oklahoma? It's a fine, private, Black college."

"You got to be kidding!" he scorned. "These little, old Black schools can't do nothing for athletes like me."

"How about offer you a strong racial support system in which to earn your degree, to be socially fulfilled, and to make a contribution to your people?"

"Hah!" James scoffed, glancing back at the game. "Get real, Doc. I'm in the spotlight and in the big time. You know how many TV games we gonna play this year? These little old Black colleges can't help me get to the pros. Plus, they can't give me a brand-new sportscar and keep my pockets full of dough. As far as being socially fulfilled is concerned, hell, my woman does that. And shit, what if I don't get a college degree? Who needs it with the bucks I'll be making?"

"Yeah, Daddy," Cynthia agreed. "I don't see *anything* wrong with wanting to make as much money as you can. Because it's money that turns the wheel of fortune. And you can be happier, more successful, and able to do even *more* for your people if you have money. Look at how much Auntie gives. And look at Black Super-star entertainers. Many of them give an awful lot of money to Black organizations."

"Well, looks like you two have it all figured out," the doctor replied.

"We do!" James boomed, hugging Cynthia.

She smiled and looked at him in admiration.

"Well, if you all will excuse me," the physician sighed, "Let me go see how Mae's coming and if she needs any help."

James returned to the game, and Ulysses looked at Cynthia as she leaned forward, circled her hand behind her head and swept her long, beautiful hair forward over one shoulder. Watching her, his pulse quickened and he took a deep breath to calm his racing heart, realizing that she was more than the sum of everything he had ever dreamed of in a woman.

"So what are you majoring in?" he asked excitedly.

"What the hell is it to you, Man!" James seethed under his breath. "Why don't you button your lip! Can't you see I'm trying to watch the game?"

Cynthia slapped his arm. "Now, don't be rude, Baby. That's bad form. I'm majoring in business," she replied.

As Ulysses glanced at her gorgeous legs, her skirt riding up to mid-thigh, he began to smolder as the room went hot all of a sudden. He had not thought to take off his jacket when he came back.

The doctor now returned, rubbing his hands together. "Boy are we gonna feast this morning. Mae's killed the fatted calf."

"That's good!" James boomed and patted his stomach. "I can always chow down!"

"Yeah, he eats like a horse, Daddy," Cynthia said.

Her father chuckled.

"Gotta keep up my strength for the pros." James sat glued to the tube again, then jumped up and hollered at a touchdown play. "Good God! Man, those Miami Dolphins are something else! That's the team I want to go to. Shit, they steamrolling everybody this year. The Raiders ain't got a chance! Whew! Damn! You don't follow football, do you, Doc?" he roared, riveted to the tube.

"No, not really. Don't have the time."

"That's too bad." James shook his head. "You don't know what you missing."

Ulysses lit another cigarette.

"Man, why don't you go outside with that smoke?" the gridder fanned the air, scowling at Ulysses. "Shit, you gonna give us all lung cancer!"

The youth smiled.

"Well, James," Dr. Johnson said, playing peacemaker, "the future sure looks bright for you, Son. And just think, after your pro career is over, you can probably go into movies and make another bundle."

"Yeah, like Jim Brown," James exclaimed. "Just think, baby. You and me starring in a movie together."

"Oh, my! What would it be?" She turned to Ulysses. "What kind of movie do you think we would look good in?"

He crossed his legs, drew on his cigarette, and glanced thoughtfully at the ceiling. "How about *Beauty and the Beast,* or better yet — *King Kong.*" He blew smoke rings.

James jumped up and hollered, "I'm sick of your ass, sucker! I'm gonna knock you out!" Ulysses jumped up, too.

"James, please!" Cynthia pleaded.

"Boys, please!" the doctor cried.

"Oh, no! I'm busting his butt! He been asking for it ever since we got here. Get outside now, wise-ass, or we gonna tear this house up! I mean it!"

Mae ran in. "What's going on?"

"I said outside!" James raged.

Ulysses quickly went out the front door with James on his tail.

Chapter Seventeen

When he got outside, Ulysses noticed some kids playing across the street and an old couple two houses down pulling a big Lincoln into their driveway. He wiped the sweat and tried to swallow, but his throat was too tight with fear.

Damn! I'm in trouble now, he thought, his heart racing. Why did I spout off like that? It just popped out. Shit, I can't whip this big ape! I'm in for a royal butt-whipping now, but I'm gonna fight him, just the same. He girded himself.

"Around to the back!" James demanded.

"James, stop it this instant!" Cynthia cried, and grabbed him.

"Get away from me!" He pulled his arm loose and quickly followed Ulysses.

When they got around to the large private backyard, beautifully landscaped with flowerbeds, and fruit, cedar, fir trees, the gridder snatched Ulysses around and tore into him. Unable to fend off the power and ferocity of the attack, the youth took a heavy blow to the nose that snapped his head back. He then saw red and felt crushing pain as he staggered backwards, pouring blood from his nose. Seeing three images of James coming at him, he felt as though his nose were broken.

"Nobody flirts with my woman, insults me, and gets away with it!" James snarled and hit Ulysses again in the face. This time the blow took him off of his feet and sent him sprawling on his back.

"You ain't never gonna forget this ass-whipping, punk!" the gridder bellowed.

Through heavy, benumbing pain, Ulysses could hear people hollering. He then cried out and curled up as he felt the point of James's shoe dig into his ribs. Such a violent stab of pain shot through him that he felt as though he were going to heave up his guts and die. Hanging onto the very edge of consciousness, he very nearly passed out.

"That'll teach you a lesson, you smart-mouth punk!" James blustered, as Dr. Johnson ran over to the youth and Cynthia jumped up and down screaming. Through the dark depths of his pain, Ulysses heard Mae shouting.

"Get away from my house! And don't ever come back!"

"He asked for it!" James shouted back. "The wimp asked for it!"

"I said leave my house at once! Or I'll call the police! I mean it!"

"You should teach him some manners, then!" James yelled.

"You've got the nerve to talk to me about manners, you barbarian?" Mae cried.

"Oh, James! James!" Cynthia put her hands to her face and wept. "What have you done!"

"I ain't done nothing to be sorry for!" he barked.

Digging deep down into his guts and snarling in pain and rage, Ulysses grabbed a handful of dirt from the flowerbed and reached the other hand into his jacket pocket, lacing his fingers through the brass knucks.

"Come on, Son. Can you stand?" the doctor asked, helping him.

"I'm okay," he seethed, struggling to his feet and breathing deeply to clear his head and shake off the pain.

"No, Son! No!" the doctor pleaded, trying to restrain him. Breaking away, Ulysses shouted at James. When the bruiser turned, the youth threw dirt into his face. James cursed and brought his hands up to his eyes, and Ulysses kicked him in the groin. When the gridder hollered and dropped his hands to his crotch, Ulysses hit him in the face with the knucks. James then cried out as the blow spun him, and he hit the dirt, heavy, bloody, and unconscious.

Everybody stood stunned as Dupree slipped the knucks back into his pocket.

"Oh, Lord! Oh, Lord!" Mae cried as the youth stood reeling on his feet, covered with blood, and Cynthia kneeled over her boyfriend in near hysterics.

"My God!" Dr. Johnson moaned. "Mae, take him inside and clean him up. I'll see after James."

"When he comes to, you get him out of here!" Mae demanded. "I mean it! And, Cynthia, don't you ever bring that animal back to my house again as long as you live, because he's not welcome! Do you hear me?"

She looked up through a veil of tears and shook her head.

"Come on, my boy. Let me help you," Mae soothed, getting her arm around Ulysses.

Chapter Eighteen

Mae fussed over Ulysses in the bathroom as she cleaned him up. "That big ape! Hurting my boy like this. You're your mother's boy, but from now on, you're my boy, too. You understand?" He nodded his head and smiled, in spite of the pain. "You've won my heart, Son, because I've never seen anybody fight with that kind of courage before. And courage is something that I greatly admire. You knew you couldn't whip that big gorilla when you fought him, but you didn't back down one bit. No, Sir. That takes sand. Because ain't many men would have stood up to him, let alone picked themselves up from the beating that you took to dish out some of their own. I'm mighty proud of you, Son, you know that?" she exclaimed. "Kind of puts me in mind of my late husband when we were kids. He was gutsy, too. Didn't let nobody push him around. I like that. And he was about your size and just as good-looking and smart. From now on, you're gonna be my boy, just like Moses became the son of Pharaoh's daughter. And you'll have a son's portion of everything I own."

"Oh, no, Mae. I couldn't."

"Yes!" she insisted. "I mean it!"

"All right! Thank you. Thank you from the bottom of my heart!" he uttered.

"That's all right," she smiled, embracing him. "I know I ain't making no mistake *this* time! You showed me more today than I could have seen in a lifetime!" She then kissed him on the forehead. "Now go on and change. It's a good thing you're wearing a leather jacket, huh? The blood came right off, didn't it?" she smiled. "Your face is gonna swell, though, that eye is gonna be black, and you'll have a bad bruise on your side. But I got something for it. How do your ribs feel? Think anything's broken?"

"I don't think so," he replied, though he felt pain whenever he took a deep breath.

"You think you need to lie down and rest a bit?"

"No, Ma'am. I'll be all right."

"You sure?"

"Uh-huh."

"Good. Then come on down after you change. No sense in wasting all that breakfast I've prepared," she grinned. "Are you up to eating a little bit, maybe?"

"I think so," he smiled back.

Chapter Nineteen

As Mae, Dr. Johnson, and Ulysses sat down to a breakfast of homemade biscuits, bacon, eggs, grits, and coffee, they talked.

"Where's Cynthia?" Mae asked. "As if I didn't know."

"She lit out of here after James like a lovesick goose," the doctor sighed. "You sure knocked the fight out of him though, Son. You've got grit, and boy can you hit. You know that?"

Ulysses smiled and ate slowly because of his pain.

"I think you gave him a lot to think about, too. As far as Cynthia is concerned. . . ." Dr. Johnson dropped his head and shook it.

"All right, so why don't you say it?" Mae uttered.

"Say what?"

"You know very well what I mean. What you've wanted to say for a long time, but never have. . . ."

"And what's that?"

"That because of my lifetime of money-grubbing, I've created a beautiful but empty shell, a materialistic and shallow butterfly."

"You said it, I didn't," the doctor replied, sipping his coffee, with a twinkle in his eye.

"You didn't have to," his sister replied, looking off

thoughtfully. "Maybe in time, I can undo some of the damage I've done. I've already tried, but it's like she's set now in concrete. But — she's still young. Maybe it's still not too late. What do you think?"

"Perhaps not," her brother sighed, eating his eggs. He then reached over and gripped his sister's hand and his face softened. "but I, too, must share the blame in this matter, Sis. I've been so busy helping others that I have neglected my own daughter. Sometimes I think you and I both, being driven people, went too far, but to opposite extremes. The ancient Greek philosophers were right — all things in moderation. One cannot give all to his people. He must give some to his family. But one must not give all to his family, either. He must also give some to his people. There is a balance there to be struck. . . ."

"Yes," Mae nodded thoughtfully. "But that can sometimes be a very difficult thing to do. I mean, how do you pursue a thing all your life and not lose yourself to it? And once lost, how do you find your way back? That's the trick. Anyway. . . ." she threw up her hands.

"But Cynthia's a very kind person!" Ulysses spoke up. "And the most beautiful girl I've ever seen."

"Oh, ho, ho! Now, do you think so?" Mae chuckled.

"Yes," he blushed and dropped his head. Mae and her brother smiled. "Excuse me. I need to step out back and get a breath of fresh air. I feel a little light-headed."

"Maybe you need to lie down, Dear," Mae suggested, as the doctor examined him.

"No, I'll be all right. If I feel like it, I'll lie down when I come back in. But you all finish eating. The breakfast is delicious, Mae."

"Thank you," she beamed.

When Ulysses stepped out the back door, he stood on the patio, gazing across the big, beautiful backyard. The sun was out, and it warmed him against the chilliness of the noon hour. Looking up and feeling pain in his face, he thought of Sammy and Mo, and also felt pain in his heart now as he watched the tall cedars gently swaying against the deep blue, cloud-flecked sky. As boys growing up together, they often had talked about all of the exciting things they would do in life. And now. . . . Tears came to his eyes, and he wiped them away, taking several deep breaths to clear his head. For a time, he did not think, but when he did, Cynthia drifted back into his thoughts, followed by another kind of pain in his heart.

CHAPTER TWENTY

After dinner, Mae, Dr. Johnson, and Ulysses sat around the living room talking. The weather had turned colder that night, and the wind had begun to howl through the trees. But inside, a toasty fire snapped and crackled in the fireplace. Christmas carols played low in the background as Mae sat crocheting a beautiful afghan.

"Doc, have you read Washington and Dubois?" Ulysses asked.

"Oh, yes! Have you?"

"No, my high school didn't offer Black history."

"Well, there are libraries, you know."

"Yeah, I know," the youth smiled. "I just never got around to checking out the books."

"No need to go to the library," Mae said. "I have their complete works upstairs in my study."

"Good!" Ulysses beamed. "Were you much influenced by them, Doc?"

"Most definitely. To be Black in America is to be immensely influenced by what those great educators had to say."

"Why is that?"

"Well, because between them, they addressed about

every aspect of the Afro-American experience during their time, which was the early part of this century. And most of what they had to say is still relevant today." Dr. Johnson sipped a glass of port.

"What did they say that most influenced you?"

"Oh," the doctor cut his eyes thoughtfully at the ceiling, "they disagreed on many points, mind you — more points than not — but they both believed that individual wealth should not be acquired by our people and used solely for selfish purposes, but should also be used to help uplift the race. And secondly, they believed that the educated ones of us should not think that we are better than the masses of Black people, and thus cut ourselves off from them."

"What should the educated do?"

"Use their education to help uplift the masses by providing political leadership and education, as well as vocational training. And then, just like the wealthy, help provide social as well as economic support for our people. You see, both of these leaders believed that money and education were two of the most important tools in building a future for the black man in America. But, of course, these resources are necessary for the rise of any people."

"I see. That's like you and Mae."

"How do you mean?"

"Well, like I work at Ken's Barbecue Pit, right?"

"Yeah."

"Well, he told me that Mae loaned him the money to start his business when no loan company would. And she also makes political campaign contributions to Black candidates and gives a lot of money to the church, charities, and Black colleges —"

"But I wasn't always that way," she interjected. "I had to learn. At one time, like many successful people, I was all for self and had selfish values. That's the part of my life that I most regret — because of my misguided influence upon Cynthia during her formative years."

"Yes," Ulysses replied. "And Doc, Mama said you help poor people get into a lot of social-service programs, and you are involved in local politics. She said that recently you helped to get some minority candidates elected to the board of education and that this will help insure that all school policies and regulations are fair and non-discriminating to minority students. Plus, you volunteer some of your time to community youth centers, to settlement houses, and nursing homes. And I know for a fact that you practice medicine in the slums, among our people, and are a friend and physician to those who can't really pay you."

The doctor smiled and nodded, and for a moment, Ulysses thought of Reverend Drew in the barber shop.

"So, you see," the doctor sipped his wine, "even if our educated and well-to-do people can't get personally involved in going that extra mile for our people, they can at least try their best to support the religious, political, educational, and social institutions that do. And together we can become a river to our people, flowing back into the Black community, and not out of it. And who knows — although perhaps we can never entirely solve the social problems that afflict the majority of African-Americans, maybe one day we can at least turn that majority into a minority. I believe, with all of my heart, that there can be no greater goal in life for any man than first to uplift himself and then to help uplift his people. But, of course, that help should extend to all men, regardless of the color of their skin."

"Yes," Ulysses smiled, and looked at Mae, who winked.

Chapter Twenty-One

Sunday morning Ulysses went to church with Mae and Dr. Johnson. He said a special prayer for his mother and Sammy and thanked God for his own abundant blessings. He also prayed that the Lord would continue to show him the right values that would enable him to properly develop as a man and be happy. And like Solomon, he also prayed for wisdom — wisdom that would lead him to the right philosophy that would enable him to make a lasting contribution to his people.

When they got home, Cynthia's car was in the driveway, and his heart leaped with joy. After they got inside, she bounded down the stairs in jeans and sweatshirt, and he noticed her beautiful curves.

"Hi, everybody!" she beamed with hugs and kisses for Mae and her father. She also had a hug for Ulysses. As he held her and felt her heavenly softness, her long silky hair, and smelled her exotic perfume, he tingled with excitement. She was bright and bubbly and exquisitely lovely, he thought. Like a beautiful tropical bird.

"Home for the holidays?" Mae asked, getting out of her coat.

"Yes," she sparkled.

"Good. Well, let's have breakfast. Cynthia, you can help

me."

"All right."

"After that I must be going," the doctor said, as they all went into the kitchen.

"You guys look so nice! Sorry I missed church," Cynthia said.

Ulysses tried not to stare at her as she moved gracefully and vibrantly about the kitchen, but it was hard, especially when she looked at him and flashed that special smile.

"How about hotcakes, everybody?" Mae asked.

The men were enthusiastic.

"Sounds great!" Cynthia exclaimed. "I can't wait to get some good home cooking for a change."

Ulysses grinned and glanced outside at the birds and squirrels flitting about in the cold, clear morning air.

"Listen," Mae asked. "What about you and James?"

"I don't know."

"What do you mean?"

"We haven't really talked since he left here. You really hurt him, do you know that?" She turned to Ulysses. "I think he had to go to the doctor. And what you said hurt him, too, Auntie."

"Good!" Mae uttered. "Because it hurts me just to look at him. And that cave man certainly needs to learn some manners!"

"Oh, Auntie!" Cynthia lamented.

"I mean it!"

"Honey, do you really love him?" her father asked. "Or is it just infatuation with money? Because if it's just the money —"

"I love him, Daddy! However, I must admit that the prospect of so much money is dazzling! But I absolutely won't chase after him. I've thought about that. I don't have to chase after any man."

"Good girl!" Her aunt hugged her. "Now you're showing some of your bloodline, for a change. I just wish you could find yourself another college boy who is nice, decent, and well-mannered. Because that thing will never make you happy. All the two of you could ever have at best would be a Hollywood marriage. And furthermore," she blended the batter, "we need to talk while you're here — woman to woman. I fear — no I *know* — that I have misguided you in this business about money. It's blinded you, Honey. You've just taken it too far!"

"Maybe. But I'll tell you one problem that we have already, and I don't know if we can really resolve it."

"What's that?" her aunt asked.

"He really likes girls and can't seem to keep his hands off of them. I mean they're all over him, and he just eats it up."

"Well, Honey, if that's a problem now, just imagine what it's gonna be like when he gets to the pros, if he makes it." Mae started to cook.

"Oh, he'll make it all right," Cynthia replied.

After she had set the table, she sat down across from Ulysses.

"Your face is bruised pretty bad. Are you in much pain?" she asked with a loving, sympathetic look and a hon-eyed, compassionate voice that made Ulysses melt.

"Oh, no," he smiled. "I'm okay."

"Good," she smiled back. "So, tell me what exciting courses you're taking in high school." She tossed her luxurious curls and her lovely earrings danced.

Calming his fluttering heart, he smiled and leaned back. "Well, it's not so much the courses I'm taking now as what I'm reading at home that's so exciting!"

"Oh? So what are you reading?" She caressed him with her bewitchingly beautiful eyes.

"Washington and Dubois," he replied, his heart still aflutter and his mind entangled in the web of her beauty.

"That's exciting?"

"Yes." He leaned forward. "You see, I'm learning so much that I should have learned a long time ago. But I guess it's never too late, huh?"

"I guess not," she smiled indulgently.

Chapter Twenty-Two

The following weeks were the happiest in Ulysses's life. He could not wait to get home after work to be with Cynthia because she gave wings to his heart, making him feel as though he were living out a dream. They laughed, played games, and went Christmas shopping together. And he and Mae sat in the evenings listening to her play piano. She was the most beautiful and accomplished young lady that he had ever met, and he fell passionately in love with her.

For Christmas, among other things, Mae surprised him with a brand-new, metallic, gray Camaro, just like Cynthia's. And he was struck utterly dumb and choked with joy.

He absolutely could not believe that his life wasn't a dream that he would suddenly awaken from. When his mother called and asked why he had not been home, and said that Gwen was there and wanted to see him, his heart sank because he could not bear to be apart from Cynthia for even a moment. But he would never tell her how much he worshipped her or to what extent he was wax in her hands, because she had made it clear that she still loved James. And she called him from time to time and slipped to Tulsa on one occasion to see him briefly, unbeknown to Mae. But Ulysses kept her secret. He also knew, however, that she and Mae could not have failed to sense the way he felt, because it was as plain as the constantly adoring look in his eyes.

Unable to put off seeing his family any longer, on Christmas day, after exchanging presents with Mae, Cynthia, and Dr. Johnson, Ulysses gathered his gifts together and drove home with a heavy and guilty heart. He also noticed, to his surprise, that the longer he stayed away from home, the more unwilling he was to return to the crime-ridden city. But especially returning to his slum environment now filled him with a kind of depression and dread that he never had imagined he could feel. After all, this was where his mother lived. This was his home.

It was a cold, dreary evening as he pulled into the alley behind the house. Collecting his presents, he walked into the back yard but stopped suddenly as a strange premonition came over him. Looking up into the trees, he saw the torrents of wind howling and whipping through the branches against the dark overcast sky.

Tree limbs creaked and snow flurries danced through the air as a quilt of decayed leaves blanketed the yard. Startled by a rattling and banging of the dilapidated garage door behind the house, he froze, suddenly hypnotized. And as he gazed at the back of his own run-down home, suddenly an illusion swirled before him. It was a ghostly theatre-in-the-round of some bizarre dream that loomed up out of the long lost past. As his vision misted over, he saw what appeared to be ghosts, romping through the air. But then they formed themselves into shades of children, playing on a bright, sunny day. They played in the great old memoried pecan tree in the backyard, and yes. . . . now he saw them clearly! Himself, Mo, and Sammy in the pecan tree, shaking down nuts, and Gwen on the ground gathering them in a basket.

* * *

"There's a lot on that limb, Mo. Shake those down," she cried.

"That limb's too far out," he objected.

"Yeah, he's too fat," Sammy grinned, as he and Ulysses continued shaking limbs.

"I ain't neither," Mo retorted.

"Please, Mo," Gwen begged. "That limb really has a lot on it."

"You think I can make it, U?" Mo fidgeted.

"Sure," he answered, without looking.

"Oh, all right," Mo conceded.

"See? He do anything for her," Sammy griped.

"Shoot! You do more for her than me," Mo exclaimed, edging out on the limb. "Give her your candy and everything when she sweet-talk your ass."

"That's a lie! At least I ain't give her all my best marbles like you did, Sucker!"

"Yeah, but you give your best slingshot to Ulysses. Look how long it took you to make that."

"Aw, forget you!" Sammy cried.

"Forget you, too, Sucker!" Mo tossed his hand just as the limb cracked. When he hit the ground, he screamed and grabbed his broken leg.

Gwen ran to him as her brother and Sammy scrambled down from the tree.

* * *

Ulysses came to himself as the wind moaned and the snow whipped his face. Shaking off his trance and feeling a heavy pain in his heart, he looked around, dazed. He could see the other back yards down the line, lying bleak and forelorn through the heavy curtain of late-evening snow. And for a moment, he imagined that he saw a graveyard some distance away, as the wind wailed like a lost soul. As he peered harder, he also could have sworn that he saw a big, black dog, tied with a chain, shivering in the cold near a headstone. Gathering himself with a shudder and taking a deep breath, he hurried toward the house.

CHAPTER TWENTY-THREE

When Ulysses unlocked the backdoor and let himself in, a toasty blanket of warmth enveloped him, as the delicious aroma of food hung in the air. He smiled at his mother, who was cooking Christmas dinner, and his sister, who was sitting talking to her, and they exploded with joy. Helping him with his presents, Gwen carried them into the living room and put them under the tree. Then she rushed back and joined her mother in hugging and kissing her brother.

"What happened to your face, Son? Are you all right?"

"I'm fine, Mama. I'll tell you all about it," he smiled.

"Just look at you!" Gwen cried, admiring his beautiful white leather coat.

"My, my, my!" his mother beamed at his fine clothes.

"He went away a poor boy and has come back rich!" Gwen exclaimed. "Hail the conquering hero!" She flourished her arm. "Returning home in triumph."

"Oh, no!" he blushed.

"May I take Your Lordship's coat?" She curtsied, as he laughed and got out of it.

"Where's your suitcase, Son?" his mother asked.

"Oh, it's out in the car. I have a new car, too, Mama!"

"What!" she exclaimed.

"What kind is it?" his sister cried, jumping up and down.

He told her.

"Oh, my! That's an *expensive* sportscar!" She put her hands to her mouth. "I want to see it. I'll get your suitcase!"

"Well, the car's covered with snow," he smiled, gazing at his mother, who was speechless.

"That's all right!" Gwen exclaimed, taking his keys and hanging up his coat. She then grabbed her own coat and dashed out the backdoor.

"A lot has happened, hasn't it, Son?"

"Yes, Ma'am, in a way."

They gazed lovingly at each other.

"Want some coffee? I got some fresh."

"Yes. That'll be nice."

"Well, sit down. Dinner will be ready in a bit."

"All right."

As the wind howled and rattled at the windows, his mother waited on him. He looked around the homey little kitchen that seemed smaller and dingier than ever. But there was also a cozy warmth about it that he loved.

Gwen then came rushing back in, breathless and shaking the snow off.

"Oh, Mama!" she cried. "You should see it! I ain't never seen anything that fine! Oh, U!" She looked at him, flabberghasted.

He smiled.

"Oh, Mama. You got to see it!"

"I'll see it," she said calmly.

Gwen took the suitcase into his bedroom, got out of her coat, then hurried back and sat down.

Mrs. Dupree poured her son's coffee and took a seat.

"Now, tell us all about it!" Gwen cried, brushing down her wind-blown hair and clapping her hands. And for the next hour, Ulysses told them everything that had happened since he had been away.

"Didn't I tell you it could happen, U?" His sister shoved him. "Didn't I tell you? And you thought I was crazy! And now look at you. An educated gentleman in the making."

He threw his head back and smiled. "What's wrong, Mama?" he asked, as she got up to see about her cooking.

"Oh, nothing. I'm just happy for you, Son."

"No, there's something wrong. Sit down, Mama, and tell me."

Mrs. Dupree returned to her seat after she checked on the turkey.

"So this woman — this Lady Bountiful — has taken you for her son, huh? Like Pharaoh's daughter took Moses? Well, where does that leave me — like Jochebed, Moses' mother? If so, then I've lost a son."

"What do you mean? You're my mama. And you always will be."

"Maybe." She looked off.

"What do you mean, maybe?"

"This Cynthia . . ." Mrs. Dupree said.

"Yes," Ulysses blushed and dropped his eyes.

"Oooh! He's got it bad!" Gwen uttered. "Oh, Mama! He's in love with her. You can see it!"

"No, I'm not," he lied.

"Yes, you are!"

"What does she look like, Son?" his mother asked, with a twinkle in her eye as Gwen smirked.

He cleared his throat and tried to control his voice as he described her in the most matter-of-fact terms. But he knew they could see through him. Ulysses felt weak and shaky at just the mention of Cynthia's name, and he struggled to maintain his composure.

Mrs. Dupree laced her fingers before her. "She's a very

beautiful girl."

He didn't say anything.

"But she's Dr. Johnson's daughter, right?"

"Yes, Ma'am."

"And Mrs. Hatcher took her and raised her for her own, gave her everything, and put her values into this child, right?"

"More or less," he shrugged, sipping his coffee.

"Uh-huh. Well, what's to stop her from taking you from me, too, and doing the same thing? I can't do for you what she can. I can't buy you all these nice things, and I wouldn't if I could."

"Oh, Mama," he dropped his head.

"Ruining you. That's what she's doing. Just like she's done that child!"

"Oh, Mama!" Gwen pleaded. "That ain't so! Don't spoil U's good fortune! He's been so blessed! You should be happy for him!"

"Yeah. But I know what you think about money, too, Gwen! And I ain't trying to spoil nothing!" Mrs. Dupree retorted. "I just don't want nobody buying my boy's love away from me and ruining him before he's had a chance to develop into a proper man."

"Mama, ain't nobody doing that!" he objected.

"No!" Gwen agreed.

"Then why ain't you been home more often?" Mrs. Dupree asked. "And why I got to call you and tell you to come home? Why, Son?" He looked down and didn't have an answer.

"You still working after school?"

"Yes, Ma'am."

"Well, that's something. Pull your own weight, Son. Be like Dr. Johnson. You gonna be so beholden to this woman and so dependent on her until she'll own you. You'll never be your own man! And won't have a nickel's worth of character to boot!"

"Oh, Mama, she ain't that kind of person at all, and I ain't gonna turn out like that. She's already admitted her mistakes in raising Cynthia."

"What do you know about what kind of woman she is? You still wet behind the ears. You don't know the ways of slick, old, cagey, rich women! Just wait till you make her mad and see how she treats you then. Heck, that old woman can buy anything she wants. And now she want to buy and ruin my boy!" Mrs. Dupree started to cry.

"Oh, Mama, don't!" Ulysses pleaded, coming around the table, kneeling, and hugging her. "Wait until you meet her before you pass judgment. She's not that kind of person at all. I promise you!"

"Meet her? I ain't never gonna meet her! What I want to meet her for? It's enough she got you!"

Gwen looked at her brother sympathetically.

"Pretty soon you ain't gonna come home at all, are you? 'Cause I know Gwen ain't when she leaves. She already made that clear. We ain't never gonna be no Ruth and Naomi. But I never thought you'd turn out to be a prodigal son. I thought you was different!" Mrs. Dupree wept. "I never thought I'd lose you, too!"

"Oh, Mama, you ain't lost me! And never will! I'd come back tomorrow, if it was safe," he lied.

"Sure you would," she uttered.

"I mean it!"

"Don't spoil Christmas, Mama!" Gwen urged. "Please!"

"I won't," she sighed, drying her eyes on her apron, and getting control. She then took a deep breath and let it out slowly. Ulysses could hear the tremor in her breath. "I won't spoil Christmas. What little time we got together means too much. You all forgive me. I'm just an old woman who's afraid and jealous, I guess. I'm all right now, though," she smiled through her tears as they smiled back. "Enough of this. Y'all forgive me, okay?" She patted her son's hand.

"Ain't nothing to forgive, Mama," he said, resuming his seat, but he was struck by the substance of her fears.

"All right, now help me set the table, Gwen."

"Yes, Ma'am."

"You going to college, Son?"

"Yes, Ma'am."

"That's wonderful! Which one?"

"O.S.U., I suppose."

"Why not the Black university? But . . .," she caught herself. "That's your business. What college do this Cynthia go to?"

"O.S.U." His heart fluttered.

"Uh-huh. Well, that's nice, I guess. Oh, you got a letter from Sammy."

"I did?" He brightened, but felt a stab of guilt.

"Yeah, it's in your room on the dresser. You written to him yet?"

"Uh, no, Ma'am."

"Why not?"

"Well, uh, I don't have his address."

"What's wrong? You couldn't get it from his mama? But you been busy, I know. Anyway, go read your letter," she said, putting her rolls in the oven.

"Yes, Ma'am," he sighed, dropping his head and leaving.

CHAPTER TWENTY-FOUR

Ulysses sat on his bed and read Sammy's letter. When he finished, Gwen stuck her head in the door.

"Come in," he said.

She did, and sat beside him, putting her arm around him. "Listen, Honey, don't let Mama upset you and spoil your joy." She spoke low.

He shook his head.

"We have to go on with our lives," she said. "She can't keep us forever, just like we won't be able to keep our kids forever."

"But she's afraid. I can understand that."

"So can I. That's why she really needs to re-marry, I guess. Because you can't hold onto anybody, once they grow up or move away."

"Mama remarry? Come on!"

"I mean it!"

"Got anybody in mind?"

"Maybe." Her eyes twinkled.

"Who?"

"Well, just between you and me," her lovely eyes flashed with amusement, "Dr. Johnson's been —"

"Oh, don't be ridiculous!" he cut her off.

She put her hand on her hip. "You called me ridiculous once before, remember?"

"Yeah, I know," he conceded. "But that's too cockeyed!"

"Why? Do I have to remind you that our mother isn't but fifty? And she's not at all a bad-looking woman, and still has a figure. Granted, she's old-fashioned, uneducated, and a little plump, but she's still smart, wise, and a darn good homemaker. Now, that would make her attractive to a lot of men — even educated ones! Believe me! I know!"

"I don't think so this time, Sis. That's just a little too far out. . . ."

"Maybe. But, anyway. . . ." She waved it away. "I'm so happy for you!" She kissed him on the cheek and rose. "You better come in to dinner, then we're gonna exchange presents. I can't wait to see what I got!" She rubbed her hands together.

"Okay." He grinned.

She started to leave, then turned, "Oh, by the way, I'm glad to see that you've taken another bit of my advice."

"What's that?"

"Your English is improving a lot."

"Thanks. I'm really working on it."

"Good! Keep up the good work."

"Oh, I will. Believe me! Thanks again."

"Don't mention it," she winked.

CHAPTER TWENTY-FIVE

"Mama, this is sure delicious!" Ulysses beamed, surveying the turkey, dressing, rolls, and dishes of sweet potatoes, green beans, corn, salad, and cranberry sauce. An apple pie and a lemon cake sat on the cabinet.

"Sure is, Mama," Gwen chimed in.

"Well, thank you."

Ulysses then glanced out the window at the trees and the yard next door, which were blanketed with snow as the big, thick flakes continued to fall. The wind whipped occasional sprays and flurries through the air as the snow began to glisten against the thickening of the evening.

"What more could we ask for?" he said, as Christmas carols, playing soft, warm, and low on the radio, cuddled their ears. "We're together, we have our health and strength, good fortune, and even a white Christmas. How about that?"

"You said it, Son! The Lord has truly blessed us!"

"Yes," Gwen smiled. "It's like something out of a Dicken's novel, isn't it? By the way, what did Sammy have to say?"

"Oh, he's pretty down, as you can imagine. But he says he's gonna make the best of it. And maybe if he can get out in a year on good behavior, he can find a decent job. Because he says that his family is having it pretty hard, now. Anyway, he said he'd write me more later when he got squared away. And he asked me to write to him. Tell him what I was doing and what was happening in the hood. He also said that he prayed that I would be safe. . . . Oh, Mama . . .!" Ulysses's eyes grew moist.

His mother gripped his hand.

"Why do I feel so guilty?" He stopped eating. "I can't write him about my good fortune. . . ."

"Brace up, Son, and don't be too hard on yourself for what happened," she comforted. "After all, you'd have done the same thing for him. That's the kind of friends y'all was — boon companions — like The Three Musketeers."

"Yeah, but it seems like he and Mo were always doing more for me and Gwen, though."

"I don't know. Y'all did an awful lot for each other."

"Yeah, but now Mo's dead, and Sammy's in prison. And I've been so blessed. It just doesn't seem right, somehow."

"I know," Mrs. Dupree sighed. "But we can't always understand the ways of Providence, Son. Just enjoy your blessings while you got them, and make the most of them. They ain't promised always. And when things go wrong, instead of getting upset or bitter, just remember how you've been blessed so far. And always try to accept whatever life gives you with good grace. That's about all we got in this world."

"Yes, Ma'am."

"Now, eat."

"All right," he smiled. "I don't know what I'd do without you, Mama."

"Awww!" she tossed her hand and grinned.

Chapter Twenty-Six

After dinner the house rang with the joyous exchange of presents. Ulysses gave his sister a beautiful watch and a lovely earring and necklace set. And for his mother, he had several fine articles of clothing. In return he received a handsome portable typewriter and desk lamp from his sister and a new pair of shoes, slacks, and a shirt from his mother. After the dishes were done, Ulysses and his sister settled down to several games of chess, while Mrs. Dupree read *The Bible.* Later that evening, Gwen taught her brother a new dance, and then talked long-distance on the phone, with her boyfriend, Jimmy, while Ulysses read and his mother watched an old movie on television.

The next day was sunny and warm. The snow began to melt as Ulysses took his mother and sister for a ride in his new car. They were both deeply impressed with its elegance and sportiness. And for the next two days, the youth lay low around the house because it was still unsafe for him to be there. But all the while, time hung heavy because he could not get Cynthia out of his mind and could not wait to see her again.

That Monday he said good-bye to his family and headed back to Guthrie. When he got there, Mae was at work, but Cynthia's car was in the driveway, and his heart jumped with joy. When he got inside, he did not see Cynthia and so took his bag up to his room. He then went down the hall to her room. The door was ajar, and she lay across her beautiful, white, canopied bed, with her back to him, writing a letter and listening to soft music. Watching her for a moment, he then glanced at the beautiful blond furniture that embellished her bedroom and the fine landscape paintings that adored the walls.

"Hi, Cindy," he greeted.

When she heard his voice, she jerked around and bounded off the bed and into his arms, kissing him passionately.

"Oh, God! I've missed you!" she cried.

"And I you!" he panted, enraptured with surprise.

Drawing back, she got control. "I — I've been so bored that's all, without. . . ."

"James?" he smiled.

She dropped her head and smiled self-consciously.

"Well, that's something," he grinned. "Maybe I'm making a little headway."

"Don't be silly." She dug her nails gently into his arm and blushed, as her alluring eyes flashed with mischief and fire.

He then gathered a handful of her hair as it fell over one shoulder and brought it to his face. "God, your hair smells so good! It's so soft, silky, and curly."

"I just washed it," she sparkled.

Then it hit him, and he knitted his brow thoughtfully.

"What race was your mother?"

"White. Why?"

"Oh, nothing," he smiled.

"Come on!" she exclaimed. "Take me for a ride in your new car.

"Where shall we go?"

"It's such a beautiful day. Let's just go riding!"

"All right!" he beamed, as his heart buzzed like a honey bee around a yellow daisy.

Chapter Twenty-Seven

It was a beautiful, bright, cold, and sunny Monday morning as they drove around. "I love your car!" she crowed. "It's really tricked out. It has a few more features than mine. I'm jealous," she pouted playfully.

"Don't be," he squeezed her hand. "Your car is lovely, too."

"Why are you going this way?" she asked, as he drove over to the Black part of town.

"What's wrong?"

"I never come over here."

"I want to show you where I work."

"I know where Ken's Barbecue Pit is."

"Do you ever go there?"

"Auntie does, but I don't."

"Why not? He makes awful good barbecue. Don't you like barbecue?"

"I love it, although it is fattening. And I eat it whenever Auntie buys it, but I don't come over here."

"I don't get it. Why not?"

"Why should I? It's shantytown. There's nothing over here but slums and poverty."

He shook his head and smiled. "Don't you have any friends in Guthrie?"

"A few casual ones. But they don't live over here, for God's sake!"

"Where do they live?"

"In the better part of town."

"You're a hypocrite and a snob. You know that?" he smiled.

"I'm not either!"

"Well, what do you call it?"

"U, people associate with those in their peer group, black or white. Haven't you studied sociology? You've got to have something in common with people to associate with them."

"Well, how about being Black," he said, heading back north.

"Don't be absurd!" she snapped.

"Well, how do you know what you've got in common with people until you associate with them?"

"Listen, I've gone to high school with poor kids, black and white. And nine times out of ten, they're not cultured and, for whatever reason, have no cultural interests or ambition."

"That sounds very snobbish!" he retorted. "Well, I'm from the slums, and I have cultural interests and ambition. I suppose you put me in that category, too?"

"There are exceptions. But you have something else that's very important, too."

"What's that?"

"Great prospects. Plus, you're improving yourself, and," she looked coy and hesitant, "you're not at all bad looking. Let's drive out in the country. Okay?"

"All right," he smiled, hitting the highway. "Let me ask you a question?"

"If you must," she replied and rolled her eyes.

"Would you be going with James if he didn't have great

prospects, as you put it?"

"Of course not. Why should I?"

"Then you're only after the money?"

"That's a stupid thing to say!" she countered.

"Well, what else is there for me to say?"

"Listen," she sighed. "All my life boys have thrown themselves at me, so why shouldn't I consider only those who have a lot to offer? I have a lot to offer. Why should I sell myself short? Or throw myself away on somebody that's not going anywhere, and wind up in a hole? That would be real smart, wouldn't it? I wasn't raised to be a fool, Honey. I know which side my bread is buttered on. And you need to get your head out of the romantic clouds!"

"Well, how about somebody's who's just not going as far —"

"Like you?" she sneered.

"Yeah, like me."

"Jesus! You make me sound like a gold digger or something."

"I didn't mean to." He gripped her hand again, and she jerked it away. "I suppose you think James is cultured, huh? A diamond in the rough maybe?"

"Go to hell!"

They didn't say anything for awhile as he drove through the beautiful, open countryside. The black-eyed Susans were still in bloom along the highway.

For a moment, Ulysses turned inward in thought. Are successful people like James ever wanted mainly for themselves, or just for what they represent? he wondered. When they find out the difference between the two, it can be very heart-breaking, I would imagine.

"You're mad at me, aren't you?" he asked.

"What was your first clue? No, you just bore me to tears, that's all!" she snarled.

"Sorry about that," he sighed.

After a moment of tense silence, he asked, "Why didn't you go to the Black university?"

"Why don't you drop dead!" she struck out.

He then pulled the car over on the shoulder and grabbed the back of her head. She tried to slap him, and he blocked her arm and pulled her face into his. As she struggled, he overpowered her and kissed her passionately. Soon her struggle gave way, and she yielded and kissed back. And then they were wrapped in one another's embrace. When they parted, they both looked drunk, and Ulysses felt stirred to the bottom of his soul.

"God, I hate you, you beast!" she uttered, out of breath, as her beautiful eyes danced with fire and fervor.

"I know," he sighed heavily, as they both looked away to gain control and to let their blood pressure fall.

Then after a moment, he started the car, and they were back on the highway again. She cracked the window to let in the cool, refreshing air. As they zipped along, the deep, thick, naked woods bristled up on each side of the highway. Ulysses glanced at the patches of evergreen flashing here and there through the dead thicket.

"You know just how far to go with me, don't you, you rat!" she sneered.

He chuckled. "In more ways than one. Mae and I have talked. Just like you two have. But even if we hadn't. . . ."

"Yes?"

"My mother and I have."

Brushing strands of hair from her face, she cracked a smile and looked at him with fascination.

"I know where I'd like to go," he said.

"Where?"

"Show me O.S.U."

"Okay!" she enthused.

"How far is it from here?"

"About thirty-two miles."

"Can we also swing by the Black university?"

"Sure. It's on the way."

"Great! What's it called?"

"Dubois. Just take a right up here at the intersection."

"Oh, yeah! I've heard of Dubois University," he exclaimed.

"You should have. It's the state's only historically Black college, but it's really integrated now," she informed.

"Is that right?" he answered, shooting down the highway.

Chapter Twenty-Eight

That evening Ulysses went back to work at Ken's Barbecue Pit. It was a nice, clean little drive-in and offered baked beans, potato salad, cole slaw, hot links, and hot fried apple and cherry pies, in addition to barbecued ribs. Ken, who was a tall, brown-skinned, middle-aged man, had his teenage son and daughter working there, also. Ricky was a junior in high school and Becky was a senior. All three youths served customers in the restaurant and took orders over the counter and at the drive-in window. They also washed dishes and cleaned up while Ken cooked and prepared the orders.

During a lull in business that evening, they all stood around talking.

"U, we want to have you over for dinner some evening," Ken said.

"I'd like that," he smiled, looking into Ken's lean, strong face.

"Good. Did you have a nice Christmas?"

"Oh, yes, Sir."

"Gosh! That's sure a beautiful ride you've got," Becky lit up. "Did you get it for Christmas?"

"Thanks. Yeah, I sure did." He grinned at the cute, petite, brown-complected young lady. "Did you all have a nice Christmas?"

"Just fine," Ken replied. "I suppose you went home to the city, didn't you?"

"Yes, I did."

"That's good," he smiled. "How's Edna Mae doing?"

"Oh, she's fine, Sir."

Becky put her hand on her hip. "Did that snobbish niece of hers come home for the holidays?"

"Be nice, Honey," her father said.

"Yeah, she came home," Ulysses replied.

"Boy, that girl is something else," Ricky shook his head and rolled his eyes.

"What do you mean?" Ulysses smiled at the likeable, husky, big-eared youth.

"She thinks she's God's gift to the world. She won't speak for nothing, Jack."

"I'm telling you!" Becky curled her lip. "I don't know where she gets off. . . . How do you take her?"

"Sometimes she's a bit much," Ulysses smiled.

"A bit much! That's an understatement!" Becky retorted.

"Well," Ken said. "Edna Mae is sure nice."

"Well, ain't none of it rubbed off on that — prima donna," Becky sneered.

"Yeah, she wouldn't give us the time of day or set foot in our place if her life depended on it," Ricky said.

"Are you kidding!" Becky rapped out. "She thinks she's too good for Black people period, just because that so-and-so is off-white. Somebody ought to —"

"That's enough!" Ken snapped. "I didn't raise y'all to talk about people behind their back."

"Shoot! I'll tell that hussy to her face!" Becky snarled, rocking on one hip.

"Come on. Enough of this. Back to work. Here come some customers," Ken said.

As Ricky took an order at the window and Becky served some patrons in the restaurant, Ulysses sat at the cash register and watched her momentarily. She was sure cute, he thought, and had a very sexy figure in her tight pants. But boy was she feisty! When she saw him looking at her, she smiled, and he smiled back. He knew that she liked him and probably wondered why he hadn't asked her out. But she would never bring it up. For a moment, he wondered, too.

He knew that he was going to need a date for the prom and with Cynthia having gone back to James, perhaps he had found her. In any event, Becky was definitely worth getting to know better.

Chapter Twenty-Nine

The next morning Ulysses and Mae sat at coffee in the kitchen. Cynthia was a late sleeper and had not come down.

"So you saw O.S.U. and D.U. yesterday, huh?" Mae asked.

"Oh, yes, Ma'am."

"What did you think?"

"O.S.U. is enormous. God, I'd get lost there."

"Until you learned your way around."

"But D.U. is nice and small," he said. "And it's a very attractive campus, too."

"Yes," she replied, as the doorbell rang. "I'll get it. I'm expecting a visitor."

When Mae returned, a tall, slim, intellectual-looking gentleman was with her. He wore glasses and a three-piece suit and looked to be in his middle thirties.

"Ulysses, I'd like for you to meet Dr. Frank Osborn. Frank, this is the young man I was telling you about, Ulysses Dupree."

The youth rose, and both men shook hands.

"Pleased to meet you, Sir," Ulysses said.

"The pleasure is all mine, Mr. Dupree," he smiled.

"Have a seat, Gentlemen," Mae uttered. "Frank, may I

get you some coffee?"

"Yes, Ma'am," he replied, crossing his legs.

Ulysses was struck by the refined, intellectual air about the gentleman as Mae set the cup before him.

"Thank you," he said.

"I wanted you two to meet," Mae remarked. "Frank is a professor at D.U."

"I see," Ulysses replied. "What do you profess, Sir?"

They laughed.

"I teach mathematics, and I understand that you're interested in pursuing that major in college."

"Oh, very much so."

"Good!" he smiled, sipping his coffee. "You know it wasn't so many years ago that I graduated from high school. But I didn't have the money to attend college. And Mrs. Hatcher gave me the money to complete my B.A. degree, because she saw something in me. Now, it would have been a great blessing if she had *loaned* me the money, because nobody else would or could. But she *gave* me the money! You understand, of course, what I'm saying," he smiled.

"Oh, yes, Sir!" Ulysses exclaimed. "I don't know why I'm surprised, though."

Everybody chuckled.

"After completing my B.A. degree, I then had the ability on my own to acquire my M.A. and my Ph.D. degrees. But had it not been for this bridge at the crossroads of my life that initially saw me across. . . ." He got up, leaned over, and hugged and kissed Mae. "I owe her a debt I can never repay."

"You owe me nothing," she answered.

Ulysses smiled warmly.

"Since then," Mae said, "he has made an indelible mark on academia by distinguishing himself like you would not believe — with awards, publications, citations, you name it. But do you know what?"

"What?" Ulysses asked excitedly.

"Big schools like O.S.U. have wooed him from all over the country, trying to get him to come to their universities and teach. They have offered him tremendous salaries and every other incentive imaginable, but he has remained at D.U."

"Why?" Ulysses asked.

Dr. Osborn adjusted his glasses. "You see, Mr. Dupree, if the best black teachers do not hold fast in their commitment to black institutions — small ones like Dubois, because that's what most of them are — the quality of their degree programs will suffer. Black schools and colleges will become increasingly weaker until a degree from them will no longer be competitive."

"I see."

"But a related issue that I might make mention of here involves Black educators in general. You see, they are becoming an endangered species. We desperately need more of them in the ranks of elementary, secondary, and higher education. Black youth are simply not becoming teachers in sufficient numbers, any more, to meet the needs of African-American students on all levels of education across this country."

"Why not?"

"Mainly because of the pay, I would imagine. Now that other more lucrative fields are open to them, minority freshmen are entering those fields. The result? A desperate shortage of Black instructors — especially in the college ranks. Even students that acquire B.A. and M.A. degrees are not going after the Ph.D."

"Why is that?"

"Again, I would imagine because of a feeling that the degree is not cost-effective, given the magnitude of effort and sacrifice required in attaining it."

"I see," Ulysses said thoughtfully.

"But again, I cannot overemphasize the fact that minority students, throughout the American educational system, desperately need teachers of their own race. They need teachers who have the ethnic as well as cultural insight, caring, understanding, and background to best deal with their peculiar problems and needs and to properly motivate them and serve as role models. Any more, when schools lose a Black instructor, there is a high probability that he will not be replaced with another African-American teacher. If this trend continues, you can well imagine that our students may be overlooked and discriminated against even more so than they are today — having no faculty representation to look out for their welfare, interests, and rights. And eventually, even our historically Black institutions may come to lose their traditions and identity through infiltration of non-Black instructors and administrators. And we must not let this happen to the institutions that have been the time-honored bastions of the educated black community and the key to its having turned out so many fine high school and college graduates, over the years."

"Boy!" Ulysses exclaimed. "How can we prevent this?"

"Well," Dr. Osborn and Mae exchanged smiles, "I say that it starts with young African-American students like yourself who understand the problem and take a personal stand to correct it in the interest of their people. You see, it always comes down to the individual."

"I see."

"Another problem is that whereas one would, of course, make a living as a teacher, there is little likelihood that he or she would ever make a lot of money in this field, relative to other professions. Teaching now, more than ever, is mostly a labor of love, a cultural and professional commitment."

"I understand."

"To help you decide whether or not D.U. is right for

you, when I get back to campus, I will send you an information packet that will tell you all of the ways that the university can help you to meet your personal, academic, and financial needs, should you, of course, decide to attend it. Then you will have a basis for comparing our school with others you may be interested in."

"Thank you, Sir," Ulysses smiled. "I would appreciate that very much."

"My pleasure," Dr. Osborn smiled back, then turned to Mae, and they talked for awhile. Eventually, he looked at his watch and said that he had to be back on campus shortly for an important meeting. "By the way, how's that beautiful niece of yours?" he inquired.

"Oh, she's just fine," Mae smiled.

"Well, good. Tell her I said 'Hi.'"

"I sure will. And thanks so much for dropping by, Frank."

"My pleasure, Mrs. Hatcher," he smiled, and they hugged. He then shook hands with Ulysses and left.

"So what do you think?" Mae asked as she and the youth sat back down.

"It's a lot to think about," he replied.

"You might be wondering why I asked Frank to come and talk to you, Son. Especially after the way I talked when you first got here."

"Oh," he shrugged and smiled knowingly.

"Well, I've been doing a lot of thinking, myself," she said. "And I don't want to make the same mistakes with you that I've made in the past. I want you to be more balanced. You understand?"

"Oh, yes, Ma'am, I do."

Mae looked off thoughtfully and knitted her brow. "In the short time since you've been here, Son, God has shown me that unless ambition and the pursuit of wealth are rooted in humane values — in helping others, especially your own people, and teaching your children the right humanitarian values — then material gain becomes an object of worship and blind, selfish, and greedy pursuit that can only lead to a life of emptiness in the end. Jesus said, 'It is easier for a camel to go through the eye of a needle, than for a rich man to enter into the kingdom of God.' And that's because most rich people worship Mammon, not God. But when the rich man becomes the philanthropist, then he has found the way to save his own soul by serving God through helping others."

Ulysses looked at her and nodded thoughtfully.

"And I've also been reflecting further on what my brother said about Washington and Dubois." Mae's face softened. "It's rather haunting, don't you think?"

"I sure do." He shook his head and smiled, and she grinned back.

Chapter Thirty

Ulysses was beside himself with happiness that last week of the Christmas holidays. He and Cynthia spent all of their time together. They rented videos of their favorite movies and danced to their favorite songs. She also tried to teach him to play the piano and tennis. And he tried to teach her to play basketball at the park. Continuing to work at his part-time job, Ulysses accepted a dinner invitation at his employer's home after work on Wednesday evening of that week.

The Mitchels lived in a modest house in the Black part of town. When Ulysses arrived, after going home to freshen up, Ken received him heartily.

"Come in, U!" he welcomed.

"Thank you."

"Are you ready to eat?"

"Oh, you bet, Sir," he replied, looking around the quietly furnished house.

"Okay. This way."

Ken then showed him into the dining room, where everyone was gathered.

"This is my wife, Tisha."

"Glad to meet you, U. I've heard some awful nice things about you." She extended her hand.

"Thank you, Ma'am!" he exclaimed, shaking hands and grinning at the short, pleasant-looking, brown-skinned woman who appeared to be in her early forties. He then greeted Becky and Ricky again as they sat at the dining room table.

"You can sit here, Son," Ken offered.

"Thank you," Ulysses replied as he sat down at the table, which was laden with food.

Ken said grace, then invited everybody to dig in.

"If you don't like chitlings, U, we got a honey-baked ham here."

"Oh, I love them!" he uttered, helping himself and looking at the dishes of mustard greens, cornbread, macaroni and cheese, sweet potatoes, tossed salad, ham, and chitlings. A German chocolate cake also sat on the table as the air hung heavy with the delicious aroma of food.

"What, no barbecue?" he joked.

"Oh, no!" Ken cried. "After cooking that stuff all day, I sure as heck don't want to come home to it."

"I can understand that," Ulysses said, as everybody chuckled.

"We just like good, down-home cooking," Ken informed. "Nothing fancy. We don't put on no airs here. We just simple country folk. Know what I mean?"

"Oh, yes, Sir!" he smiled. "Man! This is good!"

They laughed.

"Thanks!" Mrs. Mitchel beamed.

"Yeah, my wife can burn! Becky can cook, too, for that matter!" Ken bragged. "Young girls nowadays, though, can't hardly cook. That's a shame. I feel sorry for the young men."

"Yeah!" Ulysses replied as everybody chuckled and ate heartily.

"So what you gonna do after you graduate, Son? You going to college or what?"

"Yes, Sir."

"Where you going?"

Becky spoke up. "Probably to O.S.U. with that stuck-up Cynthia Johnson."

"Don't get started on her again," her father said.

"To be honest with you, I'm not sure," he informed. "Where are you going, Becky?"

"She ain't going to college," Ken replied, not looking up from his food.

Becky looked at Ulysses and dropped her eyes.

"Why not?" he asked, aware that he might be treading on delicate ground.

"No need to," Ken responded, still looking down and eating intently.

They all dined in silence for a moment.

Ken cleared his throat and looked up. "I'm trying to build a business. Pretty soon I'm gonna be branching out. There's a lot of money to be made in the barbecue business. And I ain't really got no competition around here."

He took a drink of water. "My kids are gonna help me build my business, and it's all gonna be theirs one day. Plus we gonna get us some rent houses and what not. These kids will make more money with me than they could ever make with a college degree working for somebody else. And it'll all be in the family. Plus they can avoid all that expense of college. The point behind going to college in the first place is to make money. See what I mean?"

"Oh, yes, Sir." Ulysses replied. "That makes sense."

"You darn right it does. That's what you want, too, ain't it, Baby?" Ken looked at Becky.

"Yes, Daddy." She looked up.

"Hell, my daughter don't need to go to college to continue to educate her mind. She already reads. A whole bunch of books. She reads books about great Black folks that I ain't never even heard of. You see, U, if a person wants to educate themselves, they can always do that. That's why we got libraries. But the opportunity to make a lot of money? That comes along maybe once in a lifetime, or never."

Ulysses nodded his head thoughtfully.

"Nah, U, you ain't gonna never get rich working for nobody else," Ken forked up his greens. "You got to work for yourself. And then reinvest your profits and let them work for you, too. Then you're playing on velvet. Because what that brings in is pure gravy. Pure and simple unearned income. How do you think Edna Mae got to be where she is? When she was a young woman, she started out in the restaurant business, just like me."

Ulysses nodded his head thoughtfully again as he ate with gusto.

"I want me a car like you got, U," Ricky grinned.

"You gonna have one, Son," his father said. "Just keep working hard and managing your money."

"I will, Daddy! I will!" he exclaimed.

Ken smiled, reached over, and rubbed his boy on top of the head. Ulysses smiled.

"We gonna have something, U," Ken scooped up his chitlings. "We been poor all our lives, right, Baby?"

Tisha smiled and nodded her head.

"But!" Ken grinned. "All that's gonna change. It's got to, with the whole family pulling together. But that's the trick, U. The whole family got to pull together. That's why Black folks can't get ahead nowadays, 'cause the whole family don't pull together. And Black folks don't pull together as a family. In times of war, a nation must band together as a family to survive. But so must a people when they are under constant racial siege."

"Boy!" Ulysses exclaimed.

Ken buttered his cornbread. "I only got two kids, but

some families got five or six kids or more. But the kids ain't raised right. Ain't taught the right values, and so the first chance they get, they mess up and drag the whole family down. *The Bible* says 'Train up a child in the way he should go: and when he is old, he will not depart from it.' You see, U, if a big family pulls together, with a good strong male or female at the head, ain't nothing they can't achieve. History tells us that. They don't have to stay poor. And we ain't neither. You'll see."

"I believe it," Ulysses beamed, impressed by what he heard. "But you ain't poor now." He looked around.

"Aw, this ain't nothing," Ken tossed his hand, finishing up and leaning back in his chair. "And if God ever blesses me to be worth a lot of money in my lifetime, to be in the chips, I'm gonna be like Edna Mae. I'm gonna help my people who are struggling, trying to get on their feet. 'Cause if we don't help each other, ain't nobody else gonna. And I'm teaching my kids to be the same way."

"That sounds fine," Ulysses said. "I feel the same way."

"Good!" Ken exclaimed. "If every Black person felt that way, our problems would be over, I imagine."

"I should have warned you, U. Daddy's always preaching African-American ideology," Becky said.

Ken smiled.

"You want some cake, Honey?" his wife asked.

"No, I'm full now, Baby. But a family advances just like a people do, U. With good strong leadership, pulling together financially, acquiring education or training, and sticking together and supporting each other socially. It's as simple as that. That's what Dubois and Washington always talked about." Ken shook his fist for emphasis. "The family is everything," he added. "So goes the family, so goes the nation, so go the people. If the family is torn down, then how can the nation or the people be strong?"

"That sure makes sense!" Ulysses exclaimed, and noticed Tisha smiling proudly.

Ken then got up and went into the kitchen to get a toothpick. When Ulysses glanced at Becky, she was staring at him, and he grinned. She blushed and looked away.

"Can you paint, U?" Ken asked, sitting back down and suppressing a belch.

"You mean pictures?"

"No, houses," he answered, and everybody laughed.

"Oh, yes, Sir. Fairly well."

"Good. You want to pick up some extra money this summer?"

"I sure do!"

"Good! Then I'll have plenty more work for you."

"That sounds fine!"

"That's what I like about you, Boy," Ken winked. "You hard-working and got get-up and go. Ain't a lazy bone in your body. Kids nowadays are shiftless. Want everything handed to them. But your mama sure raised you right. A man needs to always pull his own weight — even if folks are willing to do for you. They'll be all the more willing, and will respect you, to boot."

"You sound like my mother," Ulysses replied, taking a drink of tea, and they all chuckled.

"Well, good! I take my hat off to her, then!" Ken boomed. "She also taught you to be a good listener. I like that. That's awful important, you know. So many kids nowadays think they know it all. You can't tell them a thing. But old folks have a lot of wisdom. Even though they may not have any book learning or be up on the latest fads. They can still save you from a lot of pitfalls in life."

"I believe it," Ulysses replied. "I believe it."

"Baby, maybe U would like to go to church with us some Sunday," Tisha suggested.

"Yeah, U. What you think?" Ken asked.

"Oh, I'd like that very much!"

"Good! I suspect you go to church with Edna Mae every Sunday, don't you?"

"Yes, Sir, I do."

"That big Catholic church downtown?"

"Uh-huh."

"Well, we simple Holiness. Got a small church over here. But we'd love for you to come with us."

"All right." He grinned.

When he glanced over at Becky, she sat staring at him with affection.

Chapter Thirty-One

After Ulysses got home, he took a bath and lay across his big four-poster bed, listening to the thunder and the rain and writing a letter to Sammy. In his letter, he told his dear friend that he missed him a lot and would do all that he could to help him when Sammy got out. He also thanked his friend for his prayers and told his friend that God was protecting him from the Philistines. As Ulysses wrote, he looked up thoughtfully, his eyes straying across the room to the handsome mahogany bedroom suite and the beautiful pictures of nature adorning the walls.

"When someone tickled his feet, he looked around and saw Cynthia standing behind him in her pajamas. She put her hands on her hips.

"Well, did we have a special time dining with our low-brow friends this evening — especially that snippy Becky Mitchel?"

"Why you . . .!" He grabbed her and threw her on the bed. She cried out as he pinned her and kissed her. She then threw her arms around him, after which he glanced toward the door to make sure that it was closed.

"Yeah, I had a real good time. And I've been meaning to ask you, my little Passionflower. When are you going to graduate in your affection from great apes to men?"

"How dare you!" she cried, and they tussled again. When they stopped, she looked deep into his eyes. "Maybe sooner than you think. Good-night, Darling." She got up and bounded out of the room.

"Good-night," he whispered. "God, I love you so much!" he uttered as his heart trembled with excitement and backflipped with joy. Unable to continue his letter, he put it away and lay in bed, tingling with rapture and totally obsessed with his ladylove.

I'll finish my letter tomorrow, he thought. I can't finish it tonight. As he looked out at the rain, he could still smell her perfume.

Chapter Thirty-Two

The next morning after Mae, Ulysses, and Cynthia had had breakfast, the doorbell rang.

"Let's all go up to my study," Mae suggested as Cynthia went to the door and showed in a short, plump, and shrewd-looking white man, who was middle-aged and sported a nice brown suit, a briefcase, and full beard.

"Hi, Mae," he grinned, shaking hands.

"Hello, Jim. How are you doing?"

"Just fine. And you?"

"Never better."

"That's good!"

"You know Cynthia," Mae said.

"Oh, yes. How are you, Miss? As beautiful as ever I see."

"Thank you," she smiled.

"But let me present my son, Mr. Ulysses Dupree. U, this is my attorney, Mr. Jim Atkinson."

"Pleased to meet you, Sir," the youth said.

"My pleasure, Mr. Dupree. Mae, I didn't know you had a son." The attorney shook hands.

"I'm full of surprises," she grinned.

"You certainly are," he chuckled.

"Please, let's all go up to my study," Mae suggested.

"All right," the attorney replied, as they mounted the stairs.

Going down the hall, they filed into Mae's office. Ulysses looked around again at the big mahogany desk and walls lined with books. There were also file cabinets and plush, leather chairs and a sofa, along with other beautiful appointments.

"Please everyone, be seated," Mae offered.

"All right, Mae, I'll come right to the point. I know you're a busy woman," the lawyer said, opening his attache case and smoothing down his beard. "I have three cases to present to you today. The first is the second scholarship fund that you are setting up at Dubois University in the amount of $300,000."

Ulysses started, but noticed that Mae and Cynthia unfazed, sat quietly listening. Atkinson got up and came around Mae's desk.

"I have the paperwork here for you to sign. And all of the provisions you stipulated are built in. The president of the university has asked me once again to extend his most profound gratitude to you for your unbounded philanthropy. He says that he will thank you once again in person when he sees you during his business luncheon on Friday at your restaurant."

"Very good," Mae replied, signing the papers.

The attorney then filed them in his briefcase.

"The next case is a young man whom you already know, I believe. Mr. Alvin Love?"

"Oh, yes. A fine young man."

"Yes, well, Mr. Love has a small import-export business that he is struggling to launch. But to close an important deal that would really get his operation off the ground, he needs to make a business trip to Africa and stay for a month. Therefore, he seeks a loan. While there, he will finalize some important negotiations that, if successful, should yield considerable profits. And he feels certain of success. I have checked him out, and his enterprise is solid, and his prospects are good. He has, of course, tried banks but has been turned down."

"Why?" Cynthia asked.

"Insufficient collateral."

The attorney came back around Mae's desk.

"This is the amount he requests, and here are the loan papers."

"All right." Mae looked them over and signed.

The attorney then filed the papers in his briefcase.

"The third case I hesitate to bring up, and have taken the liberty of dismissing." He scratched his beard.

"What is it?" Mae asked, looking over the top of the glasses she had put on.

"This young lady sought financial assistance in setting up another beauty parlor in town. But after talking with her for only a moment, it was obvious to me that, from a business standpoint at least, she had no idea what she was doing. Plus —"

"Enough said," Mae held up her hand. "You know that I trust your judgment implicitly."

"Thank you. That means a lot," he smiled. "By the way, I also have here the current status report and financial statement from your senior citizen's foundation." He handed the document to her. "You know, Mae, you're a regular Eleanor Roosevelt, a patron saint of the poor. Without you, a whole lot of old folks around here would go under."

She took the document.

Closing his briefcase, he rose.

She rose, too. "Thanks for coming, Jim."

"It's my pleasure, Gracious Lady," he smiled, bowed, and shook hands. "I can find my way out." Nodding to

Ulysses and Cynthia, he left.

"So what do you think, U?" Mae asked, handing the papers to her niece to file and resuming her seat.

He grinned and threw up his hands. "I can't find the words. Do you do this often?"

"Are you kidding?' Cynthia replied. "I've been sitting in on these sessions since I was in high school. Sometimes they're a lot longer."

"My goodness!" Ulysses exclaimed, beaming at them. "You ever thought about opening up a bank, Mae?"

"No, Son. All banks must operate according to the laws of banking and finance. Otherwise they will fail. As a banker, I could not do what I do for people, because, in most cases, they could not qualify for the loan. But as a philanthropist, I can."

"I see," he replied.

"I asked you to sit in on this meeting because I wanted to make a point, Son."

"Yes, Ma'am?"

"Just remember, both of you," Mae held up a finger, "when God blesses you abundantly, He also blesses you to help others, all people. That is our moral obligation. Because when we have helped the least of our brethren, we have helped our Lord. And as Father Daniel always says, 'Hunger knows no race, sickness knows no sex, and nakedness knows no age.' Never forget that."

"I won't!" Ulysses replied solemnly. "I won't."

She looked at him and smiled, and he smiled back, trying for a moment to recall where he had heard those words before.

Chapter Thirty-Three

Later that morning Ulysses finished his letter to Sammy and went to mail it. After he returned, Mae's car was gone and a new, white, convertible Volkswagen sat in the driveway. When he got inside the house, Cynthia was sitting in the living room talking to a beautiful white girl who was dressed in a very elegant and sexy short, tight red dress that flaunted her lovely legs and curvaceous figure. She wore toeless high heels and had big, blue eyes and short, frosted, French-cut brunette hair. Ulysses was struck by her, and her eyes widened when she saw him.

"Hi, U!" Cynthia exclaimed.

"Hi," he smiled.

"You were wondering if I have any friends. Well, here is one. This is Michelle Leigh. Michelle, this is Ulysses Dupree."

"Hello!" She lit up, rose, and gave him her hand. "Charmed!"

"Enchanted!" he quipped, taking her hand as they all laughed and sat down.

"Do you go to O.S.U.?" he asked.

"No, I don't go to college," she gave him the eye. "I should have, though. God, it's dead around here. At least until now," she smiled and winked.

"Uh, slow down, Honey," Cynthia put her hand on her hip, "before you get a speeding ticket."

"Aren't you still with James?" Michelle asked.

"What if I am?"

"Well, some people want it all, don't they?" she winked.

Cynthia fixed her hands around Michelle's neck as they sat on the sofa looking at their high school year book. Michelle cried out and fell back as her dress rode up to her thighs.

"I think you need to pull your dress down, Michelle," Cynthia eyed her.

"Oh, yes, of course. I hadn't noticed," she smirked, rising and working her skirt down with a couple of sensual hip movements.

Cynthia rolled her eyes and shook her head.

Michelle crossed her lovely legs, and Ulysses looked away uncomfortably.

"So are you in college?" she asked.

"No, I'm a senior in high school."

"Oh, really? You seem so much more mature."

"Thank you," he smiled.

"I should have gone to college. Because this place is truly dead."

"What about Jim?'" Cynthia asked. "Aren't you still seeing him?"

"Are you kidding? I dumped that louse over a year ago."

"Why? What happened?"

"It's a long story, Honey." Michelle tossed her hand. "You wouldn't believe it. It would bore you as much as he bored me."

"So what do you do?" Ulysses asked.

"What do you mean?" she ogled, pitching her voice low and sensuous and squirming in her seat. She grinned at Cynthia.

"Geez, Michelle!" Cynthia dropped her head and shook it.

"Well, I mean what do you do for a living?" Ulysses cleared his throat and tried to control his voice.

"Well, right now I'm a bank teller," she scoffed.

"I see. That's nice."

"Sure, if you like handling other people's money. Personally, I prefer to handle my own."

"Well, Honey, you're never gonna handle a lot of it being a bank teller," Cynthia retorted.

"Tell me about it. When I passed you yesterday, Cyn, you didn't see me. I didn't know you were back in town, or I would have come over sooner. Why didn't you buzz me, Sweetie? But I know why," she leered.

"Don't be ridiculous," Cynthia snapped. "I've been very busy, that's all."

"Sure, Hon," she patted Cynthia's hand and winked at Ulysses.

In spite of himself, he was charmed and noticed that Cynthia was starting to stew.

"Would you like something to drink, Michelle? I'm afraid I've forgotten my manners," Cynthia smirked.

"I've got a better idea. Let me take you guys to lunch?"

"Well, uh, I don't know. . . ." Cynthia hesitated.

"Please! I haven't seen you in a blue moon!"

Cynthia looked at Ulysses, and he smiled and nodded. "Okay," she replied. "Just let me run upstairs and get my purse."

"Sure. Take your time, Hon."

Cynthia looked at Ulysses and rolled her eyes, then dashed upstairs. Michelle turned a hot stare on Ulysses, and he looked back at her uncomfortably. Shaking her crossed-over leg, she drew his attention back to her legs. They were firm and well-developed. When he looked up, she smiled roguishly, and he blushed.

"Hot in here, isn't it?" she observed, feasting her eyes on him, fanning herself with her hand, then wiping her hands on her skirt.

"Kinda," he replied, not looking down again. God, I wish Cynthia would hurry up, he writhed.

"You gonna be in Guthrie long?"

"For awhile."

"Good! Maybe we can get to know each other a little better."

He didn't say anything.

"Okay, everybody. Let's go," Cynthia said, bounding down the stairs. Ulysses noticed the funny look on her face.

Chapter Thirty-Four

After they got back from lunch, Michelle left, and Ulysses began cleaning out the fireplace. Cynthia kept him company.

"You need to stay away from her."

"What are you talking about?"

"I saw the way you two stared at each other and the way she gave you a leg show."

"Oh? Now look who's jealous," he smiled, scooping out the ashes and cinders into a scuttle.

"I just don't want to see you get hurt, that's all. She's on the make."

"Oh, really?"

"Really!"

"Well, just how do you think I feel about you and James? Don't you think that hurts. Or don't you care?"

"But that's not the point, is it?" she sneered.

"Oh, that's not the point? Well, I wish to hell you'd tell me what the point is!"

"I mean she's just a little floozy. You want to catch something that might be fatal?"

"Let me get this straight. You're calling your friend a tramp. Miss Prissy has trampy friends? If that's the case, then where do you get the high-and-mighty gall to downgrade decent people like the Mitchels?"

"Oh, go to hell!"

He shook his head and continued working.

"Besides, do you know who her ex is?"

He didn't answer.

"A cop. What do you think he's gonna do if he sees you with her?"

"Just let me ask you one question?"

She smirked at him.

"Are you still gonna see James?"

"I haven't sorted out my feelings yet. I told you that."

"Well, fine! Fine! I'll just sit at home, hold my breath, cross my fingers, and pray like hell — like some sappy, lovesick schoolkid with a crush on his teacher — until you get back — if you get back. And try like crazy not to imagine the good time you may or may not be having with that big ape."

"Oh, to hell with you!" she cursed and stormed out of the room.

"God!" He shook his head, tossing the coal shovel into the fireplace and coughing from the cloud of dust that rose.

Chapter Thirty-Five

Throughout the month of January, after Cynthia had returned to college, Ulysses continued going to school and working in the evenings. After work he would get his homework done. Michelle called from time to time, and he always made excuses why he could not see her. Also, he had not asked Becky out because he could not get Cynthia out of his mind and heart. Cynthia did not call him, however, and he knew why, although she did talk with Mae. One evening, to confirm his suspicion, he called her apartment, and a man answered the phone. Ulysses recognized James's voice and hung up.

"Damn!" he cursed.

Sitting in his room that night, he smoked a cigarette in the dark and stared out at the snow coming down through the street light. Then a strange thing happened. For a moment he imagined that he saw a tightrope walker, walking the telephone line and balancing with great difficulty as he extended his arms on either side of him. Rubbing his eyes, Ulysses peered out harder, through the delicate frostwork on the windows but saw nothing. Only the wind continued to moan like some creature with its back up against the glass.

Leaning back, he took a drag off of his cigarette, and tried to relax but continued to be haunted by Cynthia's beauty, her charm, her grace, and her laughter that came to his imagination like a siren song, born upon the ageless waters and the timeless winds of the past.

I wish I could undo the Christmas holidays, he thought. I might have had a chance before then. But now? He shook his head and drew on his cigarette again, letting the smoke curl from his mouth. She's in my blood. All I can do is try not to make a fool of myself over her. I mustn't beg her. It wouldn't do any good, anyway. She respects me now, but if I get down on my knees, she will despise me.

"God, help me to go on with my life!" he prayed. Putting out his cigarette, he then got into bed and dreamed of his beloved, feeling her softness, tasting her kisses, and savoring her natural fragrance.

"God, I miss you!" he whispered, staring at the ceiling and imagining that he saw her image. "Oh, Christ!" He closed his eyes and turned his face away, imagining that he held her now and that she warmed him against the cold and the wind and the snow.

Chapter Thirty-Six

Throughout February, it was bitterly cold and snowed and sleeted a lot. Ulysses went to see his mother as often as he could. On a couple of occasions, he went to church with the Mitchels. And he went rabbit hunting one Saturday with Ken and his son. Continuing to read and improve his vocabulary and English, he liked to try out new words and expressions on Dr. Johnson. The physician came over from time to time, and he and the youth engaged in philosophical discussions. But mostly Ulysses and Mae whiled away the winter evenings before the fire. They played games, watched old movies, talked, and read.

In spite of himself, however, Ulysses was looking forward to O.S.U.'s spring break. It would take place during the second week in March. And Cynthia would be home. He and Mae talked of nothing else.

During the first week in March, the severely cold weather broke. Ulysses hoped they had seen the last of the truly frigid days, as March winds rolled across the state.

On Monday evening of the following week, when he rushed home from work, he was disappointed not to find Cynthia there. She should have been there by then, he thought, as Mae sat watching an old movie. "Cynthia's not here yet?" he asked.

Mae shook her head.

"Oh," he replied, trying to hide his great disappointment.

"What are you watching, Mae?"

"Oh, it's *The Bride of Frankenstein,* Dear." Mae smiled. Struck by the emotion in her voice, he looked at her and saw that her eyes were puffy and red, and it was obvious that she had been crying. "Dinner's ready," she uttered, preoccupied, getting up and going into the kitchen.

As she helped his plate, Ulysses sat down at the table. "What's wrong, Mae?" he asked, knowing that it could not be the movie that troubled her.

"Oh, everything's all right, Dear." She tried to smile, then broke down. "Oh, U!" she wept, burying her face in her apron.

He rushed to her and sat her down, holding her as she cried. "What's wrong, Mae? What happened?"

"Oh, God! Oh, God!" she wailed.

"What's wrong?"

"It's Cynthia."

"Is she hurt?" he exclaimed.

"No. She's not hurt. But she's hurt me. She's hurt me to my soul."

"What's she done?"

"She's going to marry James."

"What!" Ulysses cried. "No! When?"

"She's marrying him over spring break. Jesus! Where did I go wrong? I've tried to do my best. God knows I've tried to do my best!"

Ulysses's eyes now gathered tears. He had lost her. And that meant the withering of his hopes and dreams for a joyful future with her.

"Oh, Lord!" he moaned, holding Mae. Why did I think

that I would ever be so lucky as to get a beautiful and wealthy girl like that, he thought, when every man who sees her, no doubt, wants her, too.

"She ain't coming home," Mae said. "I told her if she married him, she couldn't come back here, but I didn't mean it. I swear to God I didn't mean it. And she said that she wasn't coming back. Oh, U!" Mae cried. "What have I done? What have I created? Oh, what have I done to deserve this?"

"Shhhh! It's okay," he soothed. "It's okay. You haven't done anything."

"Oh, U, promise me that you will never raise your kids to worship money, because you can never undo the damage you've done!" she wailed.

"I promise! I promise!" he consoled her.

After a while, she pulled herself together.

"She's my daughter. And if I have to accept James, I will. You must, too, Son."

"I know," he groaned, continuing to hold Mae and pat her back. "I know. I'll do anything for her."

"I know you will, Dear!" she sobbed. "And so will I. Enough of this, though." She rose, drying her eyes. "Dessert's in the refrigerator, Son. But I ain't got much of an appetite!" she cried, and rushed out of the room.

Ulysses sat at the table, staring numbly into space as his eyes misted with tears.

That night he dreamed of the tightrope walker on the telephone wire again. The line stretched over a graveyard, this time. And on the graveyard below him was the big black dog he had seen in a vision before. The dog was tied with a chain and shivered in the snow. All night long Ulysses was the tightrope walker, trying to walk the line to safety. But at one point, he lost his balance and fell. However, he managed to grab onto the wire and hang by his hands. In the distance, on a barren snow-covered wasteland, he could see a dinosaur hunting for food, as the dog whimpered and lay still, hoping the creature would not see it. And all night long Ulysses tried to pull himself back up, praying that the lizard would not spot him, either. Shuddering in the snow and cold, he felt his arms grow stiff and numb as he agonized to pull himself up or swing his legs up and grab the line, but to no avail. And he was still struggling at dawn when the dream dissolved and he awakened, exhausted and sweaty.

CHAPTER THIRTY-SEVEN

The following week was also Ulysses's spring break. Trying to go on with his life, he asked Becky out to a movie, and she gladly accepted. Picking her up Saturday evening, he took her to Oklahoma City, and they stopped at a drive-in for dinner. "What would you like ?" he asked.

"I'll have a hamburger, fries, and a coke," she smiled.

"Sounds good." He ordered the same for himself, and they sat in the car and ate.

"I was wondering when you were gonna get around to asking me out," she said. "God! Your car is a dream!"

"Thank you," he smiled.

"Daddy really likes you. You know that?"

"I like him, too."

"I think he would secretly like to have you in the family."

He wanted to say, *Slow down, baby. You're going way too fast.* But instead, he simply smiled and shook his head. Ulysses then looked around at the other patrons eating in their cars.

"It's a very nice evening isn't it?" he asked, as the balmy breeze came in through the windows. "And look at that sunset! Wow!"

"It's fabulous!" she exclaimed, as they gazed at the purplish-red radiance that flamed across the western horizon. And as several large, thick, white cloud formations drifted across the sun and the hot sun rays hit them, the clouds exploded with a sunburst symphony of burnt gold, red, and blue.

"I like soft evenings like this," he said. "They're so romantic. You look very pretty tonight," he smiled, sipping his coke and looking at her pretty yellow halter dress.

"Thank you," she grinned.

Glancing at the traffic out on the bright, busy boulevard, he suddenly noticed her frowning at her hamburger.

"What's wrong?"

"This thing is not done. And I am not an Eskimo."

"Oh, I'm sorry. Maybe I can —"

"Don't bother," she uttered, wrapping it up. "Why did we come here, anyway?"

Well, uh, why not?" he shrugged, shocked at her sudden mood swing.

"This is a white place. Black people need to patronize their own businesses. That's why we have no economic power in the first place. We give all of our money to white people," she said, dumping the sandwich into the bag with disgust.

"Well, we would have had to go way to the other side of town to go to a Black restaurant."

"So what? It would have been worth it to get a decent meal."

"You're right," he sighed. "I'm sorry."

Then, after a moment, he ventured, "I get the impression that you don't care for white people very much."

"Why should I?" she bristled. "To be honest with you, I hate them."

"But why?"

"How can you ask me that?" she retorted and stopped

eating. "Why shouldn't I?"

"Oh, I don't know. Have you experienced many personal instances of racism?"

"What the hell does *that* have to do with it? But since you asked, *yes!* Haven't you?"

He jumped. "Oh, I guess so," he said, realizing that he had pushed the wrong button.

"You guess so? Don't you know? Then why would you ask me a thing like that?"

"I don't know," he sighed. "You're just so young to be filled with such hatred already."

"How old do you have to be, for God's sake? That's so silly, U! Don't you have any historical and political consciousness? Look what white people have done to us over the years, and are still doing to us. Look how they've killed off all of our leaders. You need to take a course in Black history, Honey, because it's obvious that you don't —"

"Listen," he cut her off, "I know Black history. You don't have to go off on me like that and try to put me down! Okay?"

"I'm not trying to put you down. It's just hard to believe that you read, the way you talk. So who have you read?" She sipped her coke.

Turned off, he sighed and looked away. "I've read. But it doesn't matter." The evening is shot to hell anyway, he thought. We're just not compatible, I guess.

"No, I want to know who you've read," she pressed. "Give me three authors." She looked at him cynically. "You can't, can you? That's why —"

"Oh, hell, Woman! Douglass, Washington, Dubois, King, Hughs, Wright, Ellison, Baldwin, and now I'm reading Malcolm X," he ticked them off with his fingers. "So who the hell have you read, huh?"

She looked off. "You just don't talk like you've read,

that's all."

"Why? Because I don't hate white people? I don't hate anybody, for that matter. And I've got damn good reason to hate a slew of folks. But name me one great writer, Black or otherwise, that preaches hate. And do you know why not? Because hate is self-destructive! All the great thinkers I've read talk more about cooperation and understanding, or nonviolent direct action. So if we're to be influenced by them at all, doesn't it stand to reason that —"

"Look! Do you want to go to the movies or not?" she sighed and looked at her watch. "It's getting pretty late, you know."

"Sure. All right," he snapped, tossing the trash and starting up the car.

They went to see a gangster movie, and halfway through the picture, she clasped his hand. When he did not respond, she took her hand away.

After they got back to her home, it was nearly midnight, and because they had not talked on the way back, the drive seemed to Ulysses to have taken forever. As he pulled into the driveway of her home, the house was still lighted, along with a number of others in the quiet, clean neighborhood. Looking up at the sky, bespangled with stars, and the bright, full moon that poured down its golden, yellow light, he shook his head. God! What a waste! he thought, gazing into the warm night air. The evening was astir with night sounds and aglitter with fireflies.

"Listen, I'm sorry we got off on the wrong foot," Becky said. "But thanks for a nice time, anyway."

"Sure," he managed to smile, listening to the crickets chirping and dogs barking. Somewhere deep in the darkness, a songbird was warbling, gushing out its golden, throbbing notes into the velvet night air.

When she leaned over and kissed him, the kiss left him

cold.

"By the way, all those writers that you've read are male," she said. "If you want the whole picture, you need to read some females. I might suggest Wheatley, Harper, Hurston, Walker, and Brooks, for starters. Good-night," she said and got out of the car.

"Damn!" he cursed, shaking his head and watching her go to the front door. She turned and waved, he waved back, and she stepped inside. "Shit! That overbearing bitch!" he snarled and struck the steering wheel. For a moment, he sat there, numb, staring at the moon and the stars, whose light had now grown cold.

And then he shook his head again and sighed.

Starting up the car, he drove away.

Chapter Thirty-Eight

Feeling restless and unfulfilled on such a beautiful night, he drove down the Black commercial strip, which was strung with small, seedy-looking businesses. The noisy thoroughfare pulsated and segued with sights, sounds, light, and underlife as though it were broad daylight. Ulysses moved slowly down the narrow avenue littered with trash and lined on both sides with parked cars. People came and went or just hung out, talking and looking. Some winos sat on the curb, passing around a bottle. As Ulysses crept along, he could smell fried chicken and chitlings in the air. A little further down, the aroma of fried catfish and beer assailed him.

At one point, he stopped as a man and two women argued and took their time crossing the street.

"Say, Baby," a prostitute said at his window, "what you looking for?"

"Nothing."

"You wouldn't be down here if you wasn't. You want to have a good time?"

Firing up a cigarette, he ignored her and drove on.

A cop car approached him and went by as he glanced into a couple of greasy-spoon restaurants at people eating. Easing past a row of juke joints, he heard cross-currents of jazz, blues, and boogie booming and swirling in the air. A little further down, he heard James Brown, The Godfather of Soul, belting out an oldie on the juke box.

Say it loud! Brown wailed.

I'm Black, and I'm proud! the chorus cried.

Brown wailed, *Say it loud! Unh!*

I'm Black, and I'm proud! the chorus cried.

Brown wailed, *Say it loud! Good God!*

The band exploded.

Grinning, Dupree moved on. He crawled past a storefront church where a piano was banging and a preacher was bellowing, "Though I understand all mysteries, all knowledge, and possess the world, without charity, I am nothing. You must be born again, brothers and sisters, born of the Holy Spirit, tried in the fiery furnace, and brought unto the Lord as a little child. . . ." The voice trailed off.

"Say, Homeboy," a man leaned out of the window of his parked car. "You looking for some real good dope?"

Drawing on his cigarette and letting the smoke crawl out of his mouth, Ulysses shook his head and moved on.

For an instant, it crossed his mind to get out. Was the chippy right? Was he really looking for something? If so, he didn't know what. Maybe it was just the streets that he missed — where he, Sammy, and Mo used to hang out, trying to stay out of trouble. Maybe not. At any rate, Ulysses stopped at a corner service station, gassed up, and headed home.

Chapter Thirty-Nine

Ulysses was back at Ken's Monday evening, stacking wood in the shed out back. When he finished, he ran several loads of dishes through the dishwasher and scrubbed out some heavy aluminum pots in the utility sink. Afterwards, he mopped the kitchen, took out the trash, and was momentarily caught up. During a lull in business, he and Ken stepped out back for a smoke break. Ricky and Becky minded the store.

"I never asked you, U, but how did you happen to come to Guthrie?"

"Oh," he looked out across the empty field behind the restaurant. "I had some trouble. . . ."

"What happened? If you'd rather not talk about it. . . ."

"No, it's all right," he sighed. He drew on his cigarette, and laid out the story about the Cyclops raping his sister and the revenge that he took.

"Whatever happened to Sammy and Mo?"

He told him.

"My God!" Ken exclaimed. "That's terrible!"

"Yeah," Ulysses dropped his cigarette and mashed it. He then took a deep breath of the cool, invigorating air to clear his head.

"And all this time I thought you had life pretty easy,

Son. That just goes to show you. You never can tell." Ken looked at him with admiration. "You got courage, Boy. Ain't many like you. I'll tell you that. Is your pa still alive?"

"No. Killed in Viet Nam."

"Oh, that's too bad. And your mama struggled to raise you and your sister all by herself?"

"Yeah."

"I admire her — more than I can say. She did such a fine job. I'd like to meet her one of these days."

"All right." Ulysses smiled at the feathery cirrus clouds, powdered with pastel pink, and streaking the deep, blue sky. In the west, a beautiful reddish-orange blush of sunset burned across the sun-drenched horizon.

"I used to think nobody had life harder than me," Ken ventured, lighting another smoke.

"Oh?" Ulysses replied.

"Yeah. I was raised in a little Mississippi town. Dirt poor. Big family. The Klan killed my daddy when I was just a little boy, because they said he was a troublemaker. The truth was he just tried to stand up for Black people. That's all. My mama died shortly after that."

"What happened to her?"

"Just worked herself to death, got sick, and what with grieving over Daddy. You see, they didn't find my pa for three days. It was in the dead of summer. He was shot all to pieces and left out on some lonely country road. Anyway, you know — the flies. . . ."

Ulysses looked at Ken and saw that his eyes were moist.

"I thought I could talk about it, Man, after all these years," Ken sniffed and wiped his eyes. "But it still hurts. It hurts like hell!"

Ulysses gripped his shoulder. "I understand, Brother!"

"Anyway," Ken took a deep breath, "the family was all scattered after that. I came up in one poor foster home after another. When I got old enough, I tried to join the Army, but they wouldn't take me because I have hammertoe. So I just drifted from one back-breaking, dead-end job to another, trying to stay out of trouble. But getting nowhere, because of discrimination and 'cause I didn't know nothing. It don't count for much to be young and strong in this country, U, if you Black and don't know nothing."

"Tell me about it."

"But I knew I wanted something. I knew that much. But how to get it? It was like how to get to the moon with my bare hands. Know what I mean? Times were awfully hard back then — even for whites — but especially if you was poor, Black, and unskilled, to boot. Some kids just don't know how lucky they got it these days. They throw away opportunities that their parents never even dreamed of. During the Jim-Crow era, the deck couldn't have been more stacked again us," he said.

Ulysses nodded his head.

Ken drew on his cigarette. "Then God blessed me. He blessed me in three ways. One, I met my wife, Tisha. Two, I worked for this old man in Kansas City who owned a pit, too, and made some of the best Kansas City barbecue in the world. Well, before he died, he took me under his wing and taught me his trade. Showed me the ropes — all his secrets — because he saw something in me. You know, U, there's an old saying that you can *give* a man a fish and feed him for a day, but you can *teach* a man to fish, and he can feed himself for a lifetime. That old man taught me to fish, and I'll honor him until the day I die."

Ulysses smiled.

"Anyway, armed with the knowledge of my trade, I eventually wound up here where my wife's people are. And the third way God blessed me was that when no bank would float me a loan to start my business, Edna Mae did. And I'll honor her, too, until the day I die. Because she helped to make my dream come true."

Ulysses beamed. "That's quite a story!"

"You know, U, I ain't no preacher, and I'd never try to preach to nobody. But I do know one thing."

"What's that?"

"When you want to do something with your life — something good and decent — and when you want it with all your might and when you bust your gut trying to achieve it, God will make a way for you. He will place your enemies as your footstool, make the crooked places straight, break in pieces the gates of brass, and cut asunder the bars of iron. *The Bible* says that. And it's true. Man, don't ever let *nobody* tell you that God ain't real, because He is. But each man got to find Him for himself and in his own way. Ain't nothing handed to you in this world, Son, that really and truly means anything."

Ulysses smiled and nodded. "I believe it. But what about your parents? They wanted something decent and good. And I know nobody ever tried harder. But they didn't get it."

"I know," Ken smiled thoughtfully. "*The Bible* says 'Ask, and it shall be given you; seek and ye shall find; knock, and it shall be opened unto you.' That's the way it was with me. But *The Bible* also says that Job was a good man, but for all of his goodness and faith, he was made to suffer greatly, without ever knowing why. And that's the way it was with my parents. You see, U, we can't always understand life. That's why we need faith and prayer to sustain us. Because if the primary purpose of life is to live as long as we can, then only faith and prayer can keep us going in a world that sometimes doesn't seem to be worth living in. But if life doesn't seem to be worthwhile, that's because we don't fully understand it. If we did, our minds would be as great as the Creator's. But man's understanding ain't and never will be even a rain drop in the ocean of God's understanding."

Dupree looked at him and chuckled. "Damn! That's heavy, Brother! Now, I know you didn't come to *that* understanding all by yourself."

"Are you kidding? What do I know from barbecue?"

They roared.

"No, that's what my pastor, Reverend Drew, has helped me to understand in our many talks together," Ken said. "But even if we think we understand all mysteries and think we have all knowledge, as the Reverend likes to remind us, we will always have a child's mind compared to God's, and must come unto the Lord as a little child. Otherwise, we're like a child lost from its parents. Lost in a senseless, frightening world with no comfort or security. Then what are we gonna do? But excuse me, U. Heck, I — I didn't mean to start preaching, doggone it. That's what comes of hanging around with the Reverend so much."

"That's all right," Ulysses chuckled. Where had he heard those words before?

"Anyway, we better be getting back," Ken sighed. "Oh, before I forget it. When you run a business, there's always the chance of getting robbed and killed. So I want you to know that I keep a .38 behind the check-out counter and another one in the kitchen in the drawer right next to the one with the big metal spoons. Okay?"

"Right."

"Come on." Ken grinned, embracing Ulysses.

Chapter Forty

The following week Mae said that she would try to make contact with Cynthia after her honeymoon. And that Sunday, Ulysses got together with Michelle Leigh. It was a beautiful, soft evening as he rang the doorbell at her garden apartment.

"Come in," she grinned, wearing a pair of tight, green shorts that showed off her gorgeous body.

"Thanks," he smiled, looking around the cute little one-bedroom apartment, done in blue and gold, with several beautiful oil paintings of cityscapes and skylines hung here and there.

"Can I get you something to eat or drink?" she asked excitedly.

"A coke will be fine."

"A coke!" she exclaimed. "Listen, Honey," she put her hand on her hip, "I got wine, rum, gin —"

"I don't drink."

"All right," she sighed. "Listen, would you like some — I mean, do you smoke? I got some real good weed!"

"No."

"All right," she rolled her eyes. "Please have a seat anywhere."

"Okay." He settled on the sofa.

Coming back, she set the soft drink before him on the coffee table and a stemmed glass of red wine in front of herself as she sat down beside him.

"I love your apartment," he complimented.

"Thanks," she grinned, showing her beautiful, white teeth. "I didn't think I was ever gonna get to see you, because of little, greedy Miss Johnson."

He shrugged and smiled.

"So how's she doing?"

A pained expression flickered across his face. "She's married."

"What?" Michelle exclaimed. "Why that little sneak! I don't believe it! James?"

He nodded his head.

"Why that little stinker!" she flashed a fascinated smile. "But that was a very inconsiderate thing to do to you, wasn't it?" She gripped his hand. "You must be crushed."

"I'll live."

"But it hurts, I know." She romanced him compassionately with her big baby-blue eyes.

"Yeah," he shrugged, feeling aroused by her beauty.

"So," she took a deep, excited breath and placed her hand on her breast, "that means it's open season on you, now, right? Or are you guys still gonna . . ."

"Oh, no," he laughed and took a drink. "I think you have the wrong idea about us. We were never lovers, although —"

"Oh, sure, Honey. I understand," she winked and tossed her hand. "You know I never did think she would actually marry that guy.

"Why not?"

"Oh, she's got so much class, and he's . . . Well, you know — not too cultured. But," she beamed, "he's gonna make the megabucks, and that's what our little Miss Cynthia loves, is that long green."

Ulysses frowned. "Yes."

"But enough of her. So are you seeing anybody now?"

"Not really. How about you?"

"Well, there is this guy — but, uh, the relationship can't go anywhere. I'm just passing some time. Know what I mean?"

"Sure. Is that why you're not married? Waiting for Mr. Right?" he grinned.

"Are you kidding? Mr. Right in this broken-down town? Give me a break. Unless. . . ." She looked at him provocatively.

He glanced at the beautiful cleavage that blossomed above her low-cut blouse.

"Cynthia mentioned that you used to date a cop."

"Yeah," she frowned. "Jim Lewis. God what a kink! We lived together for a while, but he got too weird for me. Sex and handcuffs and all that sort of bondage crap. Know what I mean?"

"I see," he said, realizing that this girl was much too advanced for him.

"Loosen up, Honey. You look a little tight," she said, feasting her eyes on him and sliding closer. "God, you're good-looking. I know all the girls are after you, aren't they?" She rubbed his back and arm, then brought one hand up and massaged the back of his neck.

Ulysses felt the experience in her hands as they moved with a soothing yet arousing coolness over his body.

"So do your parents live in Guthrie?" he asked, starting to feel erotic.

"Sure, why not?" She leered at his body.

"That's nice!" He stiffened.

"Uh-huh. God, you're tight. Let me give you a massage, Okay? It's sort of a hobby of mine."

"All right," he smiled.

"Let's do it this way." She sat back on the sofa and spread her legs. "Now, sit down here with your back to me."

When he did so, she pulled him back into her.

"Grab my legs," she said, wrapping them around him. "Now, lean forward and just relax. That's right."

"Oh, that's nice!" he exclaimed, as she massaged his back, shoulders, and neck.

"Uh-huh," she chuckled. "If you think *that's* nice. . . . Boy the things I could do to you!" she murmured in a hot, seductive voice. "I love the way you smell!" She kissed the back of his neck.

Holding her legs, he felt their silky softness and smelled her excitingly different body odor, mixed with perfume.

"Black guys feel so different from white guys."

"How so?" He unwound, as her skillful hands moved over him in liquid waves of delicious stimulation.

"The skin has a different texture, for one thing."

"Yes, I can tell with you," he said, rubbing her legs.

"Do I feel better than Black girls?"

"Different."

"Okay," she purred, continuing to massage him. "So what do you want to do this evening? We can stay here, if you like."

Her voice was warm and enticing.

"Well, I thought we might get a hamburger and go to the park. It's so beautiful outside, and we could walk around and —"

"Don't you want to stay here?" She bit his ear, kissed his neck, and, extending her arms under his, rubbed his chest.

He got up and sat beside her. "Gosh, I feel so much better. Thanks. You're very good at that."

Gazing intently at his mouth, she embraced him, pulled him into her, and they kissed.

"Let's stay here, okay?" she whispered. "We can order a pizza. And why don't you have a little wine? It'll help you relax. We can have a wonderful time. I *promise* you!"

"I'm all right." He pulled back.

"What is it? Are you really all right? Or is there something wrong with *me?"* She was irritated.

"No, there's nothing wrong."

"There's got to be *something* wrong! I mean, listen, are you . . ." she hesitated, "straight?"

"Yeah," he frowned.

"God, you're not making this very easy. Then what is it? Don't you want me?"

He smiled. "You're a very sexy girl, Michelle. But we don't even know each other, for God's sake."

"What's that got to do with it?"

"What's that go to do with it? Do you just jump into bed with people that you don't know even know?"

"Well, if you're afraid of AIDS, for God's sake," she rolled her eyes, "there are such things as condoms, you know."

"That's not it at all. Take AIDS out of the picture, and it's still not a good idea."

"Why not? God, you make it sound like it's such a big deal! Sex is no big deal, you know!"

"It is with me. I'm old-fashioned, I guess. It's the way I was raised. When I make love to a girl, I care. I really care. There is a commitment there. I would do anything for her, and she would do anything for me. And we would never use each other. I'm sorry. Now, if I'm wasting your time. . . ."

"No, no! It's okay, Baby. It's okay." She leaned back and gave him a strange, thoughtful look. "You're different. That's all. I've never met anybody like you."

"I don't know why not. What makes me so different?"

"What makes you so different? Well, for one thing, all

the guys I ever meet only want. . . . Anyway, come on." She jumped up, shaking her head with amused disbelief. "Let's go to the *park.*"

"All right," he grinned.

Chapter Forty-One

Almost as soon as Ulysses and Michelle had left her apartment, a cop started following them. He trailed them for several blocks, then threw on his flashers and hit his siren. Ulysses pulled over.

"Oh, God!" Michelle writhed. "That's Jim!"

Ulysses tightened as he watched the rather tall, lean, mustached officer get out and approach them, ticket book in hand. He wore sunglasses.

"What's the trouble, Officer ?" Ulysses asked.

"All right, Boy, break out some I.D. and insurance verification."

"My name is 'Ulysses Dupree,' not 'Boy'."

"Come on! Come on!" The officer snapped his fingers and made a quick beckoning motion as his face hardened. "Don't give me a hard time, Boy! Now, I didn't ask you what your damn name was!"

"Well, I'm telling you. Now, what's the problem?"

"Are you gonna give me those items or not?" The cop snarled through clenched teeth and bristled, as his hand stole to the nightstick hanging at his side.

His blood aboil, Ulysses handed over what the cop asked for and saw him looking at Michelle. She gave him a dirty look, then turned away.

Examining the documents, the cop then went back and looked at the license plate. Afterwards, he got in his patrol car and talked on the radio.

"That bastard! God, I hate him with a passion!" she seethed.

Ulysses looked at her, trying to keep his cool.

"All right, Boy," Lewis came back. "I stopped you 'cause you were weaving. Now, don't let me —"

"I was not weaving!" Ulysses retorted, glaring at him.

"That's a damn lie, you were!"

Michelle got out of the car.

"Listen, you bastard!" she threw an angry finger in his face, "I'm gonna report your ass for police harassment. That badge doesn't give you the right to go around playing Gestapo, you know! And if you're not careful, you're gonna lose it! Then what are you gonna do, you stupid son of a bitch! Everybody knows you're mad at me for dumping your ass and you'd do anything to get even. Now, you better climb down off your high horse, Mister! My parents have a hell of a lot of influence in this town. Or have you forgotten? And his mother is Edna Mae Hatcher. Now, I really don't think you want that kind of trouble! So, just back off. You got it?"

Ulysses saw him bridle, then look at her petrified. "All right," the cop swallowed. "All right. We'll — we'll let it go this time."

"You'd better let it go forever!" she shouted, with her hand on her hip.

Handing Ulysses back his license and verification, the cop turned and stalked away.

She got back in the car. "Oh, I could kill him!" she seethed.

Ulysses smiled at her with great admiration, as the cop drove away. "You're quite a fighter!" he praised.

She looked at him, and they laughed.

"I'm sorry as hell about this, U."

"That's okay. You sure took care of the situation. And how! What do your parents do, anyway?" he asked, glancing at the quiet neighborhood of nice frame and brick homes.

"My father is a criminal attorney, and my mother is a real-estate broker."

"Very impressive!" he uttered, starting up the car. As they drove through the downtown area, with its old, historic buildings, someone blew at them. Ulysses looked over and saw Ken and his family. He and Ken waved, and he noticed Becky glaring at him.

Oh, God! he thought. What more can happen?

Chapter Forty-Two

When Ulysses got back to work Monday evening, Becky would not speak to him. She stalked around the restaurant, giving him dirty looks. During a slack period in business, her father spoke to her.

"Becky, now you shouldn't act like that, Honey. After all, you and U ain't going steady or nothing. You just went out on a date once. That's all."

"Daddy, I'd expect you to take up for him, 'cause you like him so much. But he knows how I feel about white people. And he's got what he wants. Cynthia Johnson wasn't light enough for him, so I hope he's happy now."

Ulysses stood, listening.

"But, Honey, you ain't got his side of it yet."

"What side is there to get, Daddy? I mean he's got this white slut sitting all up under him. I guess he thought he'd died and gone to heaven, didn't he? Heck, he ain't no different from any other Black man, lusting after white women. Don't you ever ask me out anymore, you jerk!" she scowled, throwing an angry finger in his face. "How many women do you need, anyway? But you Black men think y'all are such studs. Well, you ain't nothing in my book, you got that?" She turned and stamped out the back door.

Ulysses dropped his head and shook it.

"Sorry about that, U," Ken sighed. "She'll eventually come around."

"Don't bet on it," Ricky said. "Becky really hates white women, Daddy. She's thinks they taking all the Black men."

"That's ridiculous," Ken replied.

"I'm going in the kitchen and have a smoke," Ulysses sighed.

"Okay, Son. I'm gonna go talk to her again. Probably won't do no good, though."

"Yeah." He shook his head.

CHAPTER FORTY-THREE

As Ulysses stood in the kitchen smoking, he sulked.

Hell, that woman acts like she owns me! Shit, she don't own me and never will. I go out with whoever I want to, whenever I want to! And to hell with her! He took a drag. She went out with me once and now wants to start henpecking and controlling my life. Well, to hell with her!

As he stood smoking, he heard some men come into the restaurant, talking loud. Ulysses very nearly had heart failure as he recognized the heavy, slow-witted drawl of the Cyclops and the deep throaty rasp of Richard Dagon.

"Jesus!" He strangled on his cigarette smoke.

"Say, Brother Man, you Ken?" Dagon boomed.

"That's right."

"My name's Richie Dagon. Me and my boys come all the way from OKC to get some of your cue. Man, you make the best damn cue in the world!"

"Damn sure do!" the Cyclops blustered.

"Well, thanks."

"I tasted some of your ribs yesterday and hollered," Dagon exclaimed. "And I wanted to know who cooked them and where could I get me some more." They cracked up laughing. "I done eat barbecue everywhere, Bro, but you the best. Can't nobody touch you! Nobody!"

"Damn sure can't!" the Cyclops drawled.

"Well, I can't tell you how pleased I am to hear that, Gents," Ken replied.

"Yes, Sir, Buddy! You sure know your stuff! We want some to eat here, Man, but we also want some to go," Dagon said. "Shit, why don't you open up a store in the city, Brother, 'cause we gonna have to keep running back here if you don't. Plus, you can make a killing!"

"Well, I hope to real soon," Ken replied.

Oh, God! Ulysses thought, putting out his cigarette and getting the .38 out of the counter drawer. He examined the gun. It was fully loaded, and he flattened himself against the wall by the doorway leading into the restaurant. There was no other way out.

"Give us seven slabs to go, Homie, with plenty of sauce," Dagon ordered.

"That's for you two, Richie, and the boys back home," Cyclops blundered out. "I want five slabs for my damn self. And make my sauce hot."

"All right," Ken replied. "Twelve slabs altogether. Is that it to go?"

"Yeah," Dagon answered. "Now, for here, give me and John Hardy here an order apiece with baked beans, potato salad, and cole slaw. What you want, Artie?"

"I want the same damn thing," Cyclops blurted out. "But just triple it. That girl there your daughter?" he asked, zeroing in on her.

"Yes," Ken answered.

Ulysses could hear the anxiety in Ken's voice now, because he knew who the men were.

"She's nice. What's your name, Baby?" Cyclops boomed.

"Becky," she quavered.

"You got a nice ass, Becky. You know that?" he gawked,

and the hoods laughed.

"Daddy, where's U?" Becky asked. "We gonna need him."

"U! U who?" Cyclops thundered. "Ulysses Dupree? I said U who? Answer me, Bitch!"

"Ulysses Morgan!" Ken exclaimed.

"You lying!" Dagon flared out. "I can look at her and tell. It ain't no Morgan, is it? It's Dupree, ain't it? I said ain't it, Bitch?"

Creeping out of the kitchen, Ulysses eased down the wall and peered around the corner into the main entrance area.

"I'll make her tell!" Cyclops bawled out, foaming at the mouth.

"I told you it's Morgan!" Ken cried. "For God's sake! It's Morgan, Man!"

Ulysses watched the Cyclops grab Becky and tear her blouse open. He grinned, and she screamed. Ken then shot him twice, the gunblasts resounding throughout the restaurant with a deafening report. As the giant slammed into the wall and crumpled to the floor, Dagon came out with his pistol, and Ulysses shot him from behind. His body pitched face forward to the floor. The other hoodlum shot Ken in the abdomen, then wheeled toward Ulysses, who shot him in the chest. The .38 hollow point took the hoodlum completely off of his feet and lunged him backwards across the floor. The air was filled with the odor of burnt oil and gunpowder.

As Becky stood screaming, Ricky kneeled over his father and hollered. Ulysses ran back behind the counter to see about Ken, but he was dead.

"Oh, God! Oh, God!" U cried, rushing to Becky.

"Daddy's dead! Daddy's dead!" Ricky hollered and cried.

As Ulysses held Becky, she continued to scream, and he slapped her. She stopped and stood trembling, with glazed-over, vacant eyes. She was going into shock.

Sitting her down, Ulysses called the police and then examined the other men. They were all dead.

As Becky sat staring at the floor, her body shook. Ulysses rushed back behind the counter to where Ricky was holding his father and moaning. Ken's eyes were closed, and he bled profusely. As the tears streamed down Ulysses's face and his stomach churned with nausea, he stood gazing into space, listening to the distant wail of sirens.

"Oh, God!" he uttered, dropping his head. "I don't believe this! Oh, Jesus! I don't believe this!" He then laced his hands on top of his head and stood gazing numbly at the floor.

Chapter Forty-Four

As Ulysses talked with the police, two ambulances came to take away the bodies. A third arrived to take Becky and Ricky to the hospital because they had gone into shock. Ulysses was allowed to go home after the police had finished their investigation and the attending physician had examined him. He was advised to immediately go home and try to rest, and to go to the emergency room at once if he started to feel very ill.

After the police and the reporters had left and the crowd dispersed, Ulysses locked up the restaurant and went home. When he got there, he told Mae what had happened, and she held him as he wept. She then put him to bed, where he lay sweating, shaking, and numb, reliving the nightmare experience and unable to get it out of his mind.

Soon he became aware of Dr. Johnson at his bedside, examining him. The physician gave him something to help him sleep.

Chapter Forty-Five

The next morning Ulysses was very depressed as he sat with Mae at coffee. She tried to encourage him and convince him that what had happened had not been his fault, any more than the death of Mo or the imprisonment of Sammy. But he could not accept it. Only after he had prayed long and hard, made confession, and received absolution in the Catholic church did he begin to feel better and pull out of his depression.

He also learned that on the evening of the tragedy, while he slept, Mae had used her influence down at the newspaper room so that when the story broke, his name and Becky's and Ricky's were left out of the report. The shooting was reported as having been an argument between the owner of a Guthrie southside barbecue pit and three known Oklahoma City gang members, and the argument had erupted into the multiple killing. Thus the existing gang members would have no one on whom to take revenge, and the three students would not be tormented with questions at school. For that, Ulysses was deeply grateful.

Chapter Forty-Six

Ulysses, Mae, and Dr. Johnson attended Ken's funeral that Wednesday. It was held in the Holiness church that Ken had belonged to, and it was heavily attended by family, friends, and relatives. So emotional was the service that Ulysses did not think he would get through it. He felt as though he would break down and go into convulsive wailing along with the family members and relatives of the deceased. But Mae and her brother were by his side, embracing, comforting, and encouraging him as he wept and mopped his eyes with a handkerchief. He managed to hold himself together throughout the ceremony.

After the graveside service, Ulysses joined the line of mourners at the cemetery. They filed past the immediate family to express their condolences. Mrs. Mitchel and Ricky returned his embrace, but when he hugged Becky, she looked at him coldly and whispered, "Because of you, my father died! Don't you ever come around us again." He drew back as though she had struck him with a knife and saw that her eyes were filled with hatred. "I'm sorry. I'm so sorry!" he whispered, moving on.

That evening, which was chilly and overcast, he went over to the Mitchels, with a heavy heart, to give Mrs. Mitchel his keys to the restaurant. When he arrived, there were many cars around the house. He rang the doorbell, and Ricky let him in. The house was full of flowers, along with relatives and friends. Ricky got his mother.

Ulysses did not see Becky. When Tisha approached him, they embraced again.

"Won't you come in, Son, and join us?"

"Would it be possible for me to speak with you a moment outside?" he asked.

"Yes, of course," she replied. And they stepped onto the front porch.

Giving her the keys, he asked if she had decided what she was going to do about the business. She said that she was going to carry on because that was her husband's dream for the family.

"Before he died, my husband set it all in place and set it all in motion, U," Tisha said, "and his death don't change nothing. Because his spirit now lives on in his family."

"That's wonderful!" Ulysses declared. He then indicated that he would love to help out, but because of the way that Becky felt, would be best if he did not. Mrs. Mitchel said that she understood, and they embraced again. With tears in his eyes, he turned and walked away.

Chapter Forty-Seven

That weekend Ulysses went to visit his mother, who greatly comforted and encouraged him. While there, he had his recurring nightmare again. It simply picked up where it had left off. The telephone line stretched as usual across the graveyard. And he hung from the line, freezing in the cold, as the big, black dog chained below shivered in the snow.

Having thought the dinosaur gone, he now saw it again when the blizzard let up. The beast moved jerkily on its hind legs and tail, perhaps a quarter mile away, in what appeared to be a frozen swamp. Looking down the wire, Ulysses could now see that it stretched over a massive stone wall as the line came out of the swamp. And the wall, standing between him and the creature, was about two hundred yards away and looked to be some twenty feet high. Underneath its coating of ice, Ulysses could see that the wall was green. But then to his utter terror, the beast spotted him and came charging. Unable to pull himself up, he hung there helplessly, waiting in horror and hollering for help, as the dog whimpered below and the lizard bounded over the wall. Suddenly, down from the sky came a gigantic bird that attacked the creature.

Ulysses watched them fight and listened to their savage battle cries of pain and fury. As they tore into each other over the icy terrain, they threw up great clouds of snow. When it was all over, the dinosaur lay dead in a great pool of blood, and the bird lay bleeding beside it, also dying. Ulysses then burst into tears. "Thank you!" he cried. "Thank you!" Just before it died, the bird raised its wing and called out to him in a loud cry, then settled into the snow. The youth continued to wail, so great was the pain in his heart. And once again, the dream dissolved.

Chapter Forty-Eight

The following week Ulysses returned to school, and that Saturday as he, Mae, and Dr. Johnson sat at breakfast, the phone rang.

"I'll get it," he said.

When the youth picked up the phone, an elderly woman was on the other end. "Is this where the parents of Cynthia Johnson live?"

"Yes."

"Well, I thought that you'd want to know about her. She's awful sick and ain't got nobody to take care of her. She looks like she's been pretty beat up, too."

"What!" Ulysses exclaimed.

"I've been trying to look after her a little, but I don't get around so good no more. I don't think she wanted me to call, but she needs looking after. And she won't eat nothing. I'm getting real worried about her. . . ."

"Wait a minute, Ma'am. Wait a minute," Ulysses stammered. "First of all, give me your address."

He jotted it down.

"Okay, now. Are you saying that she lives with you?"

"Well, she rents my little garage apartment behind my house. She's rented it for about two weeks now."

"And there's not a man with her?"

"No, Sir. She's all alone!"

"Okay, what's the best way to get to your place?" he asked, as Mae and the doctor came into the room.

The old woman told him.

"All right, Ma'am. Thanks so much for calling. We're on the way."

"Well, I thought you'd want to know. Good-bye," the woman said, and hung up.

"What is it, Son?" Mae asked.

Ulysses told them.

"Oh, my God!" she uttered. "Okay, let's go!"

Chapter Forty-Nine

As Ulysses flew down I-35 North, he drove Mae's Cadillac, and they speculated with distress about Cynthia.

"I just don't know what could have happened," Mae wrung her hands. "But it sounds like he beat her up and dumped her."

"But why would he have done that?" the doctor asked, as he rode in the front seat.

"Because he's a beast!" Mae retorted. "I told her she'd never find happiness with him."

"That just doesn't make sense, though," Dr. Johnson shook his head.

"I don't know why not," Mae replied. "How else would she wind up in this predicament, unwilling to call home? What do you think, Son?"

"I don't know," Ulysses answered. "But something happened between them, that's for sure. And it doesn't look like they got married, thank God. But if they did, he's deserted her now. I just hope to God that she's going to be all right, though," he fretted.

Mae leaned forward in the back seat and gripped his shoulder.

"So do we, Son. So do we."

It was a cool, clear, windy Saturday morning as Ulysses turned onto Highway 51 East. Moving past beautiful rolling, green countryside, they shot past tracts of budding, green woodland, herds of beef cattle, and cranking oil wells.

Keeping his eye on the speedometer, Ulysses impatiently drove the speed limit as he saw a sign ahead that said they were nine miles from Stillwater. There was moderate traffic on the highway that morning while they flew past scattered country residences, farms, and small companies.

"How do I get to this place?" he asked as they approached the outskirts of town.

"Where did she say it was located?" Dr. Johnson asked.

"She said it was on a side street called Scott, close to campus, on the north side," Ulysses replied. "She said it was off of Hall of Fame Avenue, just east of Washington Boulevard."

"I know where that is," the doctor said, as they got into Stillwater. "Turn left up here at the light."

"All right." Ulysses then took the thoroughfare that circled the north side of the beautiful, sprawling campus. Traffic was moderate as they moved past university apartments and a small campus mall on the left, and then campus buildings and the huge football stadium on the right. Stopping at two street lights, Ulysses looked at the college students coming and going.

"Okay, turn left up here," Dr. Johnson directed. "This is Scott."

Driving through the narrow, congested side street of small frame houses and parked cars, Ulysses found the address and pulled into the driveway. They saw Cynthia's car, got out, and rushed toward the little garage apartment.

Chapter Fifty

When they got inside, there was a tiny entranceway with a narrow flight of stairs. A closet full of Cynthia's belongings stood open. Quickly mounting the stairs, they passed through the little kitchen and into the bedroom. She lay facedown in bed under a thin blanket, her long, thick hair in disarray.

"Cynthia!" Mae called, staying back to allow the doctor to examine her.

He pulled the cover back, sat down on the bed, and gently turned her. All she wore was a thin nightgown.

"Oh, God! Oh, my baby!" Mae gasped.

"Oh, Jesus!" Ulysses shook his head. "Oh, Jesus!"

Her face was badly bruised, with dark circles around her eyes. She had also lost considerable weight and had a wild, wasted, worn look from illness and neglect.

"Cynthia! Can you hear me, Sweetheart?" her father held the back of her head. "She's got a pretty high fever."

"Is she going to be all right though?" Mae fretted.

"I don't know yet," Dr. Johnson replied, going into his bag.

Ulysses glanced around the room at the bare walls and few mean sticks of furniture.

"I need to examine her," the doctor said. "Could I ask

you both to please wait in the other room?" He then put on his stethoscope and took some medication from his bag.

"Yes, of course." Mae's voice shook. "Come on, Son."

They sat down at the little kitchen table that was bare except for a set of keys.

"Why don't I get her things out of the closet downstairs and load them up while we're waiting?" Ulysses suggested, looking around the little barren kitchen and feeling his heart pounding with anxiety.

As she gazed at the floor and wrung her hands, Mae looked up, dazed. "All right, Son. You know, U, I would never say this to anybody but you," she pitched her voice low. "But if this is the only way that God has given me to get my daughter back, as long as she's going to be okay, then I praise Him for it."

"So do I, Mae, so do I." He smiled and kissed her on the forehead.

Taking the keys from the table, he hurried downstairs and made several trips to Cynthia's car, loading in her clothes and several boxes of personal effects. When he finished, he stood outside and smoked a cigarette to calm himself. His hands were shaking as he glanced into the bright, clear sky and felt the cool wind on his face.

Soon Mae came to the door and beckoned him. When they got back into the bedroom, Cynthia was conscious and crying.

"She is awfully weak, but I think she's going to be all right," her father said, wiping his eyes.

Mae sat down and held her niece and they both wept.

"U is here," Mae sniffled, getting up and letting him sit down. They embraced and wept, also. He could feel her thin, frail body trembling in his arms.

"I'm so sorry! Please forgive me, everybody!" she uttered weakly.

"Oh, Cynthia!" he moaned. "There's nothing to forgive. I love you, Baby! I love you so much!"

"I love you, too!" she breathed. "I love you, too. I'm just so sorry I've been so blind and stupid! Please forgive me!"

"Shhhh. It's okay," he soothed.

"Did you and James get married, Honey?" Mae asked.

"No. And we never will! I hate him. Oh, God, I hate him so much and always will!" She exerted herself to speak in a hoarse, strained voice.

"Thank God you didn't marry him!" Mae sighed. "Did he beat you like this, Honey?"

"Yes."

"Why, for God's sake?" her father exclaimed.

As Ulysses continued to hold her, she shook with anguished sobs.

"Oh, Daddy! Oh, Daddy!" she strained, her voice whispery, as she gathered her precious strength. "I caught him and my roommate in bed together, and I — cut him."

"You did?" Mae cried. "Where did you cut him?"

"In the face. Oh, Auntie, I'm so ashamed and so — tired. Why don't you all just let me die!" she muttered, fading away. Mae turned to her brother in alarm.

"It's okay," he said. "I've given her something to help the pain and bring down the fever. It will also make her sleep. Okay, let's get her home."

"I'll carry her," Ulysses said, gathering her up and rising. She was very light.

When he got her into the back seat of the Cadillac, Mae held her.

"U, why don't you drive Cynthia's car, and I'll drive this one," the doctor suggested.

"Here's my checkbook, Son," Mae said. "Pay the landlady whatever else Cynthia owes her. And thank her again for us. Then get the rest of Cynthia's things out of the house and follow us home."

"Right," he replied, watching them leave.

He then looked up at the beautiful, cloud-flecked sky, gave a silent prayer of thanks, and started toward the landlady's house.

Chapter Fifty-One

Ulysses spent the remainder of March hurrying home after school to help take care of Cynthia. Michelle called on one occasion, and he simply explained that Cynthia was home and had not gotten married. Michelle said that she understood and wished them well. By the end of April, Cynthia was fully recovered and once again in the full flower of her extraordinary beauty and good health. By special permission from his school, Ulysses was able to take her to the prom, and they enjoyed a wonderful, magical evening together. And early in May, he graduated from high school. Since his and his sister's graduation were at the same time, Mrs. Dupree, with her son's blessing, attended Gwen's.

On the day of his graduation, Ulysses received many gifts, but the greatest was a fine banquet dinner thrown in his honor at Mae's restaurant, which was festooned in gala for the occasion. Many of his high-school friends attended and toasted him to the skies, and he likewise drank many a toast to them.

That night he had his recurring dream one last time. But this time it was utterly different. As he hung from the telephone line, gazing at the cold, cloud-crested sky, he realized that he did not have the strength to pull himself up —

so he closed his eyes and said a silent prayer that when he fell he might not die. When he opened his eyes again, the most extraordinary thing had happened. He was in the midst of a tropical paradise, with the ground just a little below his feet.

As the air hung light and cool with the delicate fragrance of exotic vegetation, flowers, and lush fruit-bearing trees, he heard the calls of brightly colored tropical birds, and spotted Cynthia beckoning to him from a nearby hillside. The hill was wooded and sloped, rising gently out of the rich, jungle-like terrain. Dropping to the ground, he ran to her, and the two lovers embraced and kissed. Then she led him to the crest of the wooded hill.

"Look!" She pointed.

And the breath went out of him in wonder as he gazed down into a beautiful, pristine canyon, bristling with trees, and boulders, and underbrush, and blazing with a symphony of greens, golds, and rusts, and the foam-laced, cool blue of the current.

"Look up there," she caught her breath, pointing to the upper course of the Congoid river, as it wound down out of the distant, thick-green highland.

"My God!" he exclaimed, gazing at the burning blue shimmer of the water, which was fed by its four major tributaries.

"Come on, let's go," she smiled, taking his hand, as the cool wind rose out of the canyon, and they disappeared into the garden forever. And once again the dream faded. But this time, because Ulysses knew that the dream was now complete, and because he somehow fathomed what it was trying to tell him, he realized that it would not return again.

The next day, which was Saturday, he took Cynthia to the city to meet his mother and sister. It was not with any sense of fear that he did so, because Dagon and the Cyclops were gone. It was also not with any sense of shame that he did so, for apart from being very proud of his family and his humble place of birth, he now noticed that Cynthia was changed. Her suffering and misfortune had somehow taken away every trace of arrogance, snobbery, and the worship of Mammon that had once marred her beautiful nature. And she was now the most exquisite and compassionate girl that he had ever laid eyes on. He could finally see that she was truly her father's child.

CHAPTER FIFTY-TWO

As he pulled the car into the alley that Saturday afternoon, it seemed to Ulysses that all of nature was abloom and was singing hymns to God's bounty. The air was warm, windy, and full of flowered sweetness. And the green trees, plants, and grass bristled and bushed with a renewed thickness and color that transformed the old alley into a homecoming paradise — or so it seemed to the ecstatic youth.

As he and Cynthia got out, he could see his mother and sister hanging clothes on the line. Relaxing in a lounge chair, Jimmy, Gwen's boyfriend, read a book under the beautifully thick, green pecan tree. Jimmy was a handsome, intellectual-looking young man of medium stature, who wore wire-rimmed glasses.

Because the clothes were flapping in the breeze and it was something of a chore to hang them, Ulysses and Cynthia were practically upon the women before they realized it. But then Gwen caught sight of them and cried to her mother and boyfriend. She then came running and threw herself into her brother's arms. Mrs. Dupree and Jimmy rushed to meet them, also.

After Ulysses and his mother had hugged and he and Jimmy had shaken hands, Ulysses said, "Cynthia, this is my mother, Mrs. Elinor Dupree, my sister Gwen, and her boyfriend Jimmy Sanders."

"I'm so pleased to meet you all," Cynthia smiled and exchanged embraces.

"And we are so pleased to meet you," Mrs. Dupree replied. "Oh, my!" she flattened her hands on her breast. "You are so lovely!"

"Oh, no!" Cynthia exclaimed. "It is your daughter that I think is so beautiful!"

"You're both knockouts!" Jimmy winked.

"I'll second that, Brother!" Ulysses beamed, and the two young men slapped five and shook hands.

"Come on, everybody, let's sit down," Mrs. Dupree smiled. "Gwen, help me get the lemonade."

"All right, Mama!" she said.

Chapter Fifty-Three

As they all sat around the back yard talking and drinking lemonade, Ulysses waved to the little kids next door playing. He then looked down the line of yards on either side of him, at the pink and red flowering crab-apple and red-bud trees splotching their vivid paints against nature's thick, rich tapestry of greens. No one else was in sight. Only birds and squirrels chirped and chattered in the trees, and the honeybees hummed among the tulips, roses, and daffodils, all in celebration of the grand rebirth of life around them. As Cynthia sat beside her beau, the wind searched her curls and brought radiance to her cheeks, while the air hung heavy with the perfumed fragrance of flowers and green pecans.

Suddenly rounding the corner of the house, Dr. Johnson and Mae appeared. And Ulysses jumped up with delight and surprise.

"When we couldn't raise anybody, we figured you were around here," the doctor smiled.

"I'm so glad you came!" Ulysses cried. "Oh, this is the happiest day of my life! Mama, I want you to meet Mae!"

"Hi, and welcome. I'm Elinor Dupree."

"And I'm Edna Mae Hatcher."

They embraced.

"I've heard so much about you," Mrs. Dupree smiled.

"And I you," Mae exclaimed.

Ulysses then introduced his sister and her boyfriend.

"Please, sit here, Mae," he offered his chair as Gwen got Mae and the doctor glasses of lemonade.

"Jimmy, how are you, My Friend?" the physician cried.

"Just fine, Sir! Oh, it's good to see you!"

"Good to see you, too, Son." And the men shook hands and hugged.

"Please, sit here, Sir." Jimmy offered his seat as he and Ulysses sat on the grass.

"What a beautiful day!" Mae exclaimed. "What an absolutely gorgeous day. And it is so lovely out here."

"Yes, it is!" Ulysses uttered.

"So how is med school, Jimmy?" the doctor inquired.

"Oh, just fine, Sir. I'm in my last year, as you know."

"Oh, yes. Where will you do your residency?"

"In D.C. That will give Gwen time to finish nursing school. Then, as you know, we're coming home, like the swallows of Capistrano. Are we still gonna build that clinic here?"

"Oh, you bet we are!" the doctor beamed.

"And I'm going to help!" Mae offered. "Anybody tries to stop me is in for a fight."

They all laughed.

"Oh, we won't try to stop you," Jimmy enthused. "We'll be eternally grateful for your help. In life we need both the philanthropist and the visionary to carry out projects of far-reaching humanitarian value."

The doctor winked and nodded as Mae smiled proudly.

"But," the physician cleared his throat. "I think you'll need to talk this over with Gwen first. She may not —"

"We've already talked," Gwen replied. "I've fought this long and hard inside myself, and, well — I've decided that whatever Jimmy wants, I want. Wherever he goes, I go."

"Oh, Baby, you don't know how happy that makes me!" Mrs. Dupree clapped her hands together.

"Yes, I do, Mama," she smiled. "Yes, I do."

"Ulysses, what about you and Cynthia?" the doctor asked.

"Well, we've talked it over, and we're going to Dubois University in the fall. She's going to continue her major in business, and I will enter the math department. I want to go straight through for my master's. And when I finish, I'll come back here and teach in my old high school for a few years. After that, I want to go on for my Ph.D. at O.S.U., and afterwards, maybe they can use me at Dubois. Who knows?"

"Oh, that sounds wonderful!" the doctor replied, and they all agreed. "What about you, Honey?"

Cynthia smiled. "I'll go straight through for my master's in business, and then we want to start a family." She took Ulysses's hand.

"How about a double wedding, then?" Mae brightened. "Now, wouldn't that be something?"

"It sure would!" Mrs. Dupree exclaimed.

"It'll be my gift," Mae said. "That and the honeymoon."

"No, *our* gift," Mrs. Dupree amended.

"No, *our* gift!" the doctor declared. And everybody laughed.

"Any idea when the weddings might be?" Mae asked.

"How about this summer?" Jimmy suggested, looking at Gwen, who nodded her head.

Ulysses and Cynthia looked at one another and smiled.

"Good!" Mae beamed. "Then it's all set. Now my happiness is complete!"

"Yes," the doctor smiled.

"I would like to say something," Ulysses cleared his throat.

They all looked at him.

"Just like James said, it takes the idealist *and* the philanthropist to carry out projects of far-reaching humanitarian value. Well, I would also like to say that it also takes family and friends. I think the greatest investment is in people though. I am living proof. God knows where I would be today without your help and the help of friends like Sammy, Mo, and Ken. And God knows where other young African-Americans like me would be today without the similar support of people like you in their lives. I can't speak for anyone else, but my happiness would certainly be far from complete. Because not only would I not have found myself, but also I would never have found the lady of my dreams, or a bright future to embark upon. And one day — I swear by Almighty God" he held up his hand, "I will also help to invest in our people — especially in our young, because they are, after all, our future. And I know that I speak for other African-Americans like myself when I say that, in the spirit of Washington and Dubois, I will help to teach these young people the right humanitarian values and help to open the doors of salvation and opportunity for them as was done for me. And they will in turn, I know, do likewise for others of our people. And my God, with that ripple effect," Ulysses smiled, "what can we not accomplish in time as a people, by the grace of God, if we hold fast to this vision always. . . ."

Everyone exploded in applause as Ulysses wiped his eyes.

"It's all about helping each other. Uplifting ourselves. Because nobody else is gonna do it for us. I just want to say thank you. Thank you all, from the bottom of my heart."

"You are most welcome." Mae beamed, amidst the cheers and applause.

"I would also like to propose a toast!" Ulysses proclaimed, raising his glass. "To Black women — to beautiful, powerful, and strong Black women who, throughout history, have been the backbone of the Black male, and without whom the Black male would truly have become an extinct species in more ways than one. Here's to Black women everywhere."

"To Black women." Jimmy cried, and they all drank a toast and again erupted in cheers.

Smiling, Ulysses looked up at the beautiful castles of cumulus clouds, drifting across the clear, deep blue sky. And as he held Cynthia's hand and they smiled deep into each other's eyes, he wonder what he had ever done in this world to have been blessed to find such happiness and fulfillment in life. But then the words of Reverend Drew came back to him: "Just always carry God with you, Young Man, and don't ever turn your back on your people, and God will heap blessings on you a hundredfold."

"Yes!" Ulysses said. "Yes!"

The End

About The Author

Jerry Evans was born in Oklahoma, where he still lives and is a college professor, holding the Ph.D. degree in English. **THE AFRICAN-AMERICAN** is his sixth novel. Dr. Evans is married and has two sons.